Brooke J. Losee

BLOOD

&

MAGIC

Children of Magic: Book 1

Brooke J. Losee

ISBN: 978-1-954136-06-9

BLOOD

&

MAGIC

Children of Magic: Book 1

CHAPTER ONE
Secrets Revealed

Magic could make quick work of thatching a new roof, but Eramus wasn't at liberty to use his hidden power. The smack of a metal hammer drove a nail into the long wooden plank next to him, fastening it to the roof with a familiar ping. Several men worked beside him and the noonday sun baked their skin, beading sweat on their faces.

Eramus swiped his jet black hair from his forehead and wiped his brow with the back of his hand. For two days now, he and his fellow villagers had been working hard to secure a new roof on Roderick's two-story cottage. The old man watched from the ground with folded arms, his body crumpled by his twisted spine. The harsh winter had done a number on the aged roof, leaving it full of holes that allowed water to seep into the interior. Hopefully after today, that would no longer be a problem.

Eramus drew in a deep breath. Though he had plenty of muscle from his work helping the local farmers and tradesmen, his arms ached from the exertion. He knew a much easier and faster method of making the repairs but could never allow himself to utilize his power—at least not with people watching. Revealing his secret would be a disaster. His people wouldn't respond well to magic, what with the hushed rumors that the army of Izarden and previous king had met their doom facing a powerful sorcerer. How much of that story was true, however, he couldn't say.

A soft voice caught his attention. Eramus peeked over the edge of the roof to see a young woman wearing a yellow dress and holding a basket around one arm. Though her brown bonnet shaded her face, he knew at once who she was. He'd recognize that voice and long braid of golden hair anywhere.

"I've brought lunch for everyone!" she called in a tone that flowed like a melody. Then again, Evree's voice always sounded like music to Eramus. "Everyone come down and take a break!"

Eramus didn't require more of an invitation. He climbed down the ladder behind two other men and eagerly waited his turn for lunch. His stomach grumbled, but he cared more about who was serving the food than what the meal would comprise.

"Good afternoon, Eramus," she said, handing him a sandwich and an apple. The way the sunlight made her green eyes sparkle twisted his stomach into a tight knot.

"Good afternoon, Evree. How are you today?"

Her lips lifted, and Eramus noted that wider smiles caused a little dimple to form on the right side of her cheek. "I'm well. Thank you for asking."

Eramus opened his mouth to say more, but the blasted words didn't come. Her brilliant green eyes had stolen them, which happened frequently, and always when others were around to watch him flounder.

Evree bit her lip. Her gaze shifted to the cottage, drawn there by the men still hammering away on the roof. "It looks like you're making wonderful progress," she said as her attention moved back to him.

He nodded, a bit too dramatically, but he needed another moment to find his voice. "Yes...yes, I'd say we are. Should have it completed by this evening."

Her smile returned, and his mind went blank. "That's good to hear. I'm sure Roderick will be happy to feel safe from the spring rains."

His head bobbed up and down while his mouth hung open.
Blast.

Eramus didn't know his exact age, but at near nineteen, he shouldn't struggle to make conversation like this. Evree left his thoughts as messy as smashed berries.

Someone behind him cleared their throat. "You know, I don't mean to sound impatient, but there's a line of hungry men behind you, boy."

Eramus was sure his face had colored, judging by the excess heat that spread through his cheeks. "Forgive me. I'll just..." He swallowed hard and stepped to the side. Evree continued to hand out food while Eramus watched her from beneath a nearby birch tree. Every once in a while, her eyes would flick to him, briefly enough that he questioned whether they had really fallen on him at all.

Once all the men had their food, Evree stepped closer to the cottage, her eyebrow raised and her arms folded. "Papa! Come down and take a break! You've been up there since sunrise. You need to eat something!"

Eramus smiled. Evree's voice was beautiful, even when she chided. How did she manage that?

Her father, Kieran, lifted his head, a drop of sweat rolling from his forehead. "All right, sweetheart. I'll be down in just a moment." Evree's grin of triumph made Eramus chuckle.

Her father moved to the edge of the roof and started down the ladder. Evree stood right below, waiting for him. As soon as his foot met the third step, a loud crack echoed through the air. Kieran yelped and his arms jerked forward to grip the edge of the roof just as the ladder fell sideways. Eramus shot towards them faster than his mind could register what his body was doing. Kieran attempted to reposition his hands, and in doing so pulled a loose board to the edge, sending it fumbling towards the ground...and Evree.

Eramus whirled his hands through the air until a bright blue light surrounded them. An enormous dome appeared over his head just as he reached Evree's side. The wooden board crashed down on top of it, and the plank snapped in two before falling to the ground.

Evree had ducked into the crevice of his shoulder, but the clonk of the wood rattling against the ground lifted her gaze. Her eyes settled briefly on him, then grew wide as they moved over his shoulder. "Papa!"

Eramus followed her gaze. Kieran had lost his grip on the roof and was dangling by one hand with just the tips of his fingers. Eramus dissipated his shield, his hands cutting through the air. A beam of energy flowed from his palms towards Evree's father and surrounded his entire body.

"Kieran! You can let go!" Eramus tried to keep his tone even, but his heart raced madly. "I've got you. Please, trust me!"

Kieran looked over his shoulder, his eyes reflecting his uncertainty. They locked on Eramus, and he gave him one strong nod of encouragement. Kieran released his hold on the roof. The blue aura surrounding his body held him in the air, suspended by what one could only call magic. Eramus willed him to the ground with the smooth motions of his hands. Once Kieran's feet found the dirt, the blue energy dissipated. Evree released a puff of air, then ran to her father and wrapped her arms around his neck.

He held her in a tight embrace, muttering into her ear. "I'm all right, sweetheart. I'm all right."

She sobbed. Eramus watched them for several long moments before the whispers caught his ears. His eyes darted to the horrified expressions watching him. What had he done? He'd spent his entire life hiding his secret. He'd told no one in the village about his *powers.* How could he? They would have questions he wouldn't be able to answer. He knew too little about himself to provide the information they would demand.

The whispers gave way to a humming murmur. His pulse quickened. They would expect answers soon, judging by their looks of suspicion. Eramus's eyes flicked to Kieran's, and found his full of question too, but there was also a softness that reflected gratitude. Eramus had saved them, but would the act be celebrated or cursed?

There was no reason to stay. His feet moved, and within seconds, he was sprinting through the village. Eramus could feel the stares on his back, piercing him like daggers of distrust. He had acted on impulse. He had saved two people from harm, or perhaps something worse, and therefore couldn't regret revealing his most tightly guarded secret, but fear gripped him like a nightmare he couldn't awaken from. His life had just become more complicated than he ever imagined.

Eramus ran along the central path of the village until he reached the stone cottage at the very end. He paused to give his racing heart time to calm. Pink flowers grew in little wooden boxes below the tiny window on the right side. The structure was small, but had an air of homeliness about it. This cottage was the only home he'd ever known...or at least remembered. His guardian wouldn't be happy about today. She'd scold him until sunrise.

He released a heavy breath through his nose. Now wasn't the time to upset Inara. He needed to calm himself down first. A light breeze tousled pieces of his black hair as he made his way to the barn behind the cottage and walked inside, leaving the door ajar. The air was stuffy, but at least he could be alone here. At least there were no suspicious eyes or deafening whispers to concern himself with.

A chestnut mare shifted in the stall a few yards away. He wasn't entirely alone, but he would receive no ill treatment from the animals sheltered inside the barn. They would never view his power as strange or scary. They would not see him as something dangerous.

Eramus held out his trembling hands. With a few seconds of focus, a blue light encircled them. The aura glistened in the sunlight that percolated through the loft window, leaving him with a sense of warmth. Magic. It was the only word he could think of to describe the phenomenon. Beyond the old story, this strange power he possessed was not something he'd ever heard of anyone else having, nor did he understand where it came from. He supposed he might have been born with his ability, but even that aspect of his life was a complete mystery to him. Perhaps if he could remember his childhood, he might find the answers.

Eramus closed his eyes and willed the light surrounding his hands to evaporate. He lay down on the floor of the barn and stared up at the ceiling. He twisted a piece of scratchy straw between his fingers, and for a long time, his mind replayed the event in his head.

"You appear lost to your thoughts, Eramus."

He sat up abruptly at the sound of Inara's voice. The woman stared at him for a moment, her mouth drawn in a firm line and her brows raised high on her forehead. The scolding...it was sure to follow.

Eramus brushed the straw from his hair and pursed his lips. "I take it you heard what happened?"

She folded her arms. She'd most definitely heard.

Eramus heaved an exasperated sigh. "I know I'm not supposed to let anyone see, but Evree and her father were in danger. What was I supposed to do?"

"You're supposed to not let anyone see!" she said, tossing her hands in the air. "Do you realize what you have done? The village is in an uproar about the whole thing! I've already had several come to me, demanding answers, which I can't even give them."

"That's not my fault!"

Her face softened, leaving a pang of guilt on his heart. Inara didn't deserve to be shouted at. None of this was her fault, either. He owed a great deal to the woman who had taken in a child with no one else to turn to. "I'm sorry. I'm not upset with you. Just with myself."

Inara's dark green dress grazed the floor as she seated herself beside him on the straw. Her fingers fell onto his arm, warming it through his clothes. He met her eyes, full of sympathy and love. *Love.* She'd loved him for the last ten years, as if he were her own son. Although Inara had no children of her own, she was a wonderful mother to him, kind and patient, even in his many boyhood antics.

"My sweet Eramus. Your heart is far too kind. I knew one day something like this would happen. You're too compassionate not to use your gift to help others."

His *gift*. That was what she had always called it. Eramus wasn't sure the word was really appropriate. Besides, if it was a gift, Inara wouldn't insist on keeping it a secret.

"I'm sorry I let you down. This whole thing will put you under scrutiny. I wished I had thought...it all just happened so fast..." His voice cracked. He suspected the fact that Evree had been the one in danger had something to do with his quick response. His actions would cause problems for both him and Inara, but Eramus couldn't bring himself to regret what he'd done. He could never regret saving someone from harm, no matter what the implications would do to him.

Inara patted his arm. "We will be fine. I knew it was bound to happen, eventually. If the people had to find out about your gift, an act of heroism isn't the worst scenario for the discovery. I do not worry about myself, but for how they will treat you. I can't fathom someone hurting you, Eramus."

His eyes stung. Inara wrapped her petite arms around his shoulders and pulled him against her chest. She was a tiny woman, and Eramus had outgrown the ability to crawl into her lap a long time ago, but she managed to comfort him all the same.

Her fingers rubbed in circles on his back. Eramus could remember nothing about his actual mother, but he imagined this was what it would be like to feel her love, to feel safe in her arms. "Everything will work out, my dear. What is life if not a bit complicated?"

Eramus chuckled at the amusement in her tone. "Complicated or not, I'm happy that I have you to share it with. Without you, I would be lost."

She took his head between her hands and lifted it to look into his eyes. "It is I who would be lost, dear. You've given me purpose all these years. You know I love you."

A smile tugged at his lips. He knew. He could never repay Inara for everything she had done. All he could give her was his smile and the words that warmed him to the depth of his soul. "I love you, too."

The barn darkened. Eramus glanced towards the tall figure standing in the door frame, their face shadowed but not enough to keep their identity unknown. He and Inara rose simultaneously.

"Arnan," said his mother. "What a lovely surprise. Have you come for a visit?"

The man took a step into the barn, his expression becoming fully visible. The sternness in his voice made Eramus's heart pound. "You know why I'm here. I intend to call a meeting, and I expect you to come. I'll send word when we are ready."

He didn't wait for a reply, disappearing back into the open air and out of sight.

"Oh, my," Inara whispered.

Eramus's gaze remained fixed on the entry. This was it; his people would demand answers. How much of his ignorance they would accept, he couldn't say. He had no choice but to attend the meeting and hope the outcome would not destroy everything he held dear.

CHAPTER TWO
Distrust & Misgivings

Eramus watched the clouds turn pink as the sun dove behind the mountains. An eventful day left him exhausted. He and Inara sat at the wooden table in the living area of their small home, finishing the last of their dinner. Besides the two tiny rooms on the eastern side of the cottage, this space held the majority of their possessions. It wasn't much, but he'd never wanted for anything.

Inara glanced at him when his fork hovered in front of his face for too long.

"How are you feeling, dear?"

Eramus sighed and dropped the utensil back to his plate. "I don't know. A storm of questions is what I expected, but we've waited all afternoon. Surely Arnan will hold the meeting soon?"

Inara nodded and placed another chunk of potato into her

mouth. "I wouldn't think on it, dear," she said after swallowing. "The others will demand answers, that is to be certain. But for now, I think it best we enjoy the quiet."

"I suppose you are right, but I can't help but feel anxious about the whole of it. I would prefer to get it over with, rather than sit in unending anticipation."

Inara watched him for a moment, her lips curling into a small smirk. "Is it the opinion of the village or one young lady in particular that has you so anxious?"

Eramus swallowed hard. How was he to answer that? Surely he wasn't so obvious that Inara had noticed? "What do you mean? What specific young lady are you referring to?"

She narrowed her eyes, suggesting she was completely unconvinced of his ignorance on the matter. "Oh, I don't know. One with blonde hair and green eyes. About your age, I should think. You might have saved her life recently."

Eramus mussed his hair and leaned back in his chair. "Why would I care what Evree thinks? She will react no differently than anyone else here."

Inara scoffed. "I should hope not. You saved her. I would expect some gratitude, at least, and hope for more than indifference if you are to court her."

A piece of potato lodged in his throat, throwing him into a fit of coughing until it came loose. "Court?" he sputtered with his hand over his mouth. "What makes you think I wish to court her?"

"Oh, Eramus, stop it! I may be old, but I'm not *that* old. I see the way you look at her, watch her like no one else exists. You've had an affection for her for some time. You should do something about it."

Eramus groaned. Was he truly so obvious? Did that mean Evree knew of his feelings as well? He could think of nothing more embarrassing.

A knock sounded at the door. A strange mixture of relief and trepidation filled his chest. Inara welcomed a young man inside. When his brown eyes fell on Eramus, the man fidgeted with his gloves and moved his attention to the back of the cottage. "Forgive the intrusion, but Arnan has called a meeting. Everyone is requested to be present."

"I see," said Inara. "And we are to discuss what happened at Roderick's cottage earlier this morning?"

The young man shifted his weight and stared at the floor. "Yes, Madam. I believe we are. You can hardly blame anyone for desiring answers. I saw the event with my own eyes." He looked up at Eramus, his eyes reflecting the turmoil of emotion below the surface. "It was quite amazing, to be sure, but I think it has left folks unsettled."

Inara turned towards Eramus, and a set of deep wrinkles formed on her forehead. Eramus stood. He wasn't sure he could give the villagers answers, but he could tell them what little he knew. He didn't want to be feared or despised. The village had been his home for the last decade. Most of the people knew him well, and he hoped they would forgive his deception.

"I will come to the meeting and do my best to answer their questions. I assure you, I mean no harm to anyone. I only desired to keep Evree and her father from injury."

The young man smiled. That was a good sign, wasn't it? He seemed to accept his answer and approve. Perhaps the rest of the village would as well.

"I suppose there is no avoiding it," said Inara, holding up her skirts as she started for the door. "I always knew this day would come."

They made their walk to the meadow in silence. Eramus focused on his breathing, hoping to calm his racing heart before they arrived, but the effort did little good. The sizable crowd sent his heart hammering with such intensity that his chest ached.

The village leader, Arnan, stood at the front, his suspicious eyes watching from beneath his thick, bushy brows. Eramus believed Arnan had always held him in high regard, but it seemed the incident this morning had replaced that respect with distrust. Eramus suspected that was the case for most of the people who were standing on the dark green grass, waiting for his explanation.

Arnan spoke with the tone of a man in charge—heavy and firm. He was not someone to be trifled with on the best of days, and Eramus sensed this situation had him in a rather foul mood. "I think we all know why we are here, and as you all well know, I don't believe in wasting time. So, allow me to proceed without formalities. Eramus, if you wouldn't mind joining me up here. We've some questions for you about the accident this morning at Roderick's cottage."

Inara patted his shoulder. Slow, even steps moved him forward as he studied the expressions of the parting crowd. He could see everything in their eyes. Some held fear, others an intense curiosity. Before he reached Arnan, his gaze found Evree's. Her lips pulled into a soft smile. His chest constricted, but he managed a nod. At least she didn't appear to hate or fear him.

Eramus stopped beside Arnan and waited for his interrogation to begin. He shifted nervously as the man's dark eyes looked him over for several moments.

"Let's start with the obvious questions, Eramus. What is this power you possess, and where does it come from?"

Eramus chewed the inside of his cheek. Why must they start with questions he had no answer for? He would have to do his best to answer honestly. Hopefully, that would be enough. "I don't know what to call this power. Some might call it magic, and I think that may even be appropriate, but others might call it a gift." He found Inara in the crowd. She beamed and gave him a reassuring nod. Eramus drew in a deep breath and continued, "As for where my power comes from, I cannot say. Everyone knows I have lost all memories of my past. I can only assume I gained this *ability* in my youth, or was simply born with it."

Whispers sounded through the air, calling his heart into a robust performance. Eramus dared to glance at Arnan, who stood with his arms folded and his brows raised high. "You're saying you've had this *gift* the entire time you've lived here?"

Eramus clenched his jaw. Answering would put not only himself under speculation but also Inara. No one would believe such an odd thing remained unnoticed by the woman who had raised and cared for him over the last ten years.

He glanced at her again, hoping she would help him know what to do. Her brows drew together, but she gave him another firm nod, encouraging him to continue. "Yes, I've possessed this gift since I came to live among you. We thought it best to keep it a secret for fear of how everyone would react."

Arnan turned to face the crowd. Eramus could no longer see the man's face well enough to follow his gaze, but he was certain Arnan was staring at Inara. He wanted to protect her from any wrath she might receive from the people. It was the least he could do after everything she had done for him. He would protect her, even if it meant he had to use his power to do it.

"I must say, I am disappointed in this deceitfulness. I thought I knew you, Eramus. But we cannot linger on it now. What's done is done. As the leader of this village, it is my duty to make sure everyone is kept from harm. I do not understand this power you possess, nor do you, it seems. For this reason, I must ask that you leave."

Voices rose from the crowd, some in whispers and others in shouts. Arnan held up his hand, and all fell silent. Before the man could continue his speech, Inara stepped forward, her eyes wide and her body tense. "Please, Arnan! You cannot ask him to leave. Where will he go? We are the only people he knows. I am his only family."

"Inara, I am sorry, but I cannot have a threat so blatant—"

Someone else forced their way through the crowd, shouting over Arnan with thunderous force. "I will not stand by while you banish the man responsible for saving my life!" Kieran rushed to join them at the front of the group, a fire burning in his eyes unlike Eramus had ever seen. He took to Eramus's side, turning to address the village with what was sure to be a fervent speech. Kieran and Arnan often disagreed on how their small community should run, which typically resulted in heated discussions. The men were very similar, in both stubbornness and appearance, characteristics attributed to the fact that they were brothers.

"Eramus has saved my life and the life of my daughter. I owe him a great debt, and I will not stand idle while his character is so abused. I ask you, since when does an act of heroism demand for banishment from our midst? My brother would have you believe that Eramus's power is a threat, but I have never seen him behave aggressively towards anyone in this village, either in word or deed. He is an honorable man, a fact none of you can deny. Do not punish him for hiding this secret from you. If today proved anything, it is that he was right to fear our reaction." He glanced at Arnan, his eyes fierce. "We should, as Eramus has so wisely stated, think of his power as a gift."

Arnan scowled, his fists balled tightly at his side. "A gift? You don't know what you say, Kieran. How do we know we can trust him? How do we know he won't use his magic against us?"

"He has lived with us for a decade! Why would he start now?" Kieran stepped closer to his brother, his words barely audible to Eramus, and certainly soft enough to escape the ears of the crowd. Kieran pushed his finger against Arnan's broad chest. "It is not this village you think he threatens, it is you. Your pride and greed will be the ruin of us all if you don't evaluate your motives, brother."

Kieran turned to face the crowd again. "I propose a vote. Eramus should be allowed that much." The muttering among the villagers sounded as though they agreed with Kieran.

"Fine!" Arnan shouted over the people. "Let us take a vote, then. All in favor of the banishment of this man and his unknown power, and the threats that could accompany such power, raise one hand."

Eramus's stomach rolled. He didn't dare count the many hands that shot towards the sky, instead choosing to close his eyes and wait for the verdict. "Forty two in favor of banishment. Now, those in favor of allowing this man to remain in our midst, please show the same sign."

The silence seemed to drag on. He couldn't bring himself to open his eyes, not until he heard the vote count for those in favor of allowing him to stay. How many people lived in his village? Why had he never taken the time to consider such a thing? It certainly would be a pleasant fact to know right now. Were there even enough people left to outnumber those who had already cast their vote?

"The vote stands at sixty in favor of Eramus remaining," Arnan said through what sounded like clenched teeth.

Eramus's eyes flew open. He could stay? The majority had voted against his banishment? The surprise outcome formed a lump in his throat. Perhaps his village wouldn't fear him as he thought they might, at least not all of them. He searched for Inara. The setting sun reflected off the trail of tears on her wrinkled cheeks. She smiled at him, but he was not naive enough to miss the fear that lingered in her eyes. She was right to have such fears. There were certainly many among them who believed Eramus should leave.

"This meeting is adjourned," said Arnan before forcing his way through the crowd.

The people dispersed to their homes. Eramus caught Kieran on the shoulder before he could leave. "Kieran, I don't...I'm not sure how I can ever thank you."

Kieran studied him for several long moments. His eyes still held a fierce fire, one that sent chills through Eramus. The man's voice was gruff and stern, filled with an unspoken warning. "Do not make me regret it."

Eramus's blood ran cold. Kieran's harsh words left him to wonder what the man truly thought of his powers. Perhaps there was more discontent among the villagers than he thought, despite the majority voting for him to stay.

Kieran guided Evree through the dense crowd. She stole one last glance at Eramus over her shoulder, her soft smile ever present.

Inara joined his side and took his hands in her own. "I've never been more scared," she whispered. "The thought of losing you..."

Eramus shook his head and hugged the woman, whose head fit under his chin when he pulled her close. "You could never lose me. You've been a mother to me all these years. Even if they sent me away, you would still have a place in my heart."

Inara pulled away and tapped her petite hand against his face. To his surprise, she smirked and repeated the pat against his skin. "You need to shave, Eramus. You're rather prickly."

His laughter made her smile stretch. "I shall see to that first thing in the morning," he said. "I'm too overwhelmed at the moment to care."

She nodded. "Come, dear. Let us go home and talk." Eramus followed her gaze to where it settled on a few villagers, Arnan included, who had yet to leave the meadow. The man's scowl deepened as he stared back at them. Perhaps Kieran was right. Arnan likely felt threatened by his abilities, and if that was true, the man would not just let this go.

"I think we've had enough public display for one day," Inara said.

Eramus squeezed her hand. "I wholeheartedly agree."

Although today had been difficult, he had a sinking feeling he was not out of the woods yet. Arnan would not make things easy for him, but to what extent the man's contempt would go was anyone's guess.

CHAPTER THREE
Recanting the Past

Crickets chirped outside the window. Night had descended on the small village, and the moonlight percolating into their cottage illuminated Inara's wrinkled face. The deep creases on her forehead and near her eyes betrayed her happy facade. Eramus had always known his secret would be discovered, but nothing could have prepared either of them for it.

Inara gave Eramus's hand a small squeeze. "Talk to me, dear. I know today was difficult. I can't imagine what you must be thinking."

Eramus sighed. "I don't know where to begin. I fear our people will never trust me again, and what kind of life would that be? Hated and despised..." He stared out into the darkness. A weight pressed on his chest, straining his lungs. Despite being granted permission to stay, his life would never be the same.

"You are neither hated nor despised. Our people know you, Eramus. They will not cast you out. The vote tonight proved that."

Eramus shook his head. "No, many of them will not, but it doesn't mean they will fully trust me, either. I feel as though I have lost something important. Having one's honor questioned is far more difficult than I ever imagined."

"Only an honorable man would find such questioning difficult." She winked, and he couldn't stop himself from smiling. "Give them time, Eramus. The people will come around. They will see you for the wonderful man you are. Your gift can help us in so many ways. They need only see the light it can bring."

"I hope you are right. I want to prove to everyone I am the same person I have always been."

"Especially Evree?"

Eramus smacked his hand against the table and scowled. "Mother!"

Her shoulders shook with laughter. "What? It's true, is it not?" She pointed at him, a sly smile stealing over her lips. "Don't think I didn't notice you staring at her, even while the entire village was watching."

He groaned and rubbed his hands over his face as she continued, "*And...I* noticed she stared right back. Couldn't take her eyes off of you."

Eramus scrunched his nose. "Of course she stared back! I was literally the center of attention at the meeting. Where else would she look?"

Inara shrugged. "Perhaps, but no one else stared at you *that* way."

He propped his head up with one fist and blinked at her. "You're not going to let this go, are you? Even if I had an...an *affection* for Evree"—he shook his head and pointed at her when her face lit up with excitement—"and I'm not saying that I do! No one would ever give me permission to court their daughter after what happened. You know they wouldn't."

She waved her hand dismissively. "Oh, don't be ridiculous. You saved her life. Kieran would be a fool not to accept your courtship."

Eramus hung his head, his palms resting flat on his forehead. Inara would not be swayed, and truthfully, his mother was right. He cared for Evree; he had for a long time. But that didn't change the fact that he had lost the trust of his people. Kieran had given him a clear warning. Eramus stood no chance of obtaining permission to court his daughter.

But now wasn't the time to concern himself with that. More important matters plagued his thoughts. He had so many questions, and although he knew Inara had always been honest, Eramus believed information lay hidden within the details of the day she found him.

He leaned forward and took her hand. "Mother, would you...I know you've told me so many times, but..."

Inara patted his wrist. "Of course, dear. What do you want to know?"

"Just start from the beginning."

She nodded, and a smile tugged at one side of her mouth. "Arnan and several women, including myself, had taken a trip to

Olgetha, a small city on the Sea of Maleze. We hoped to sell our apple harvest to the merchants at the port. After unloading the crop, we took a stroll along the shore. I remember the sky so well—dark and cloudy, the remnants of a massive storm that had devastated the area throughout the night. The waves were still harsh and the air cool. I can't imagine...if we hadn't walked the beach..."

Her eyes glazed. Eramus wrapped his fingers around her hand and she continued, "I was picking up shells. There was a small cove where they would get trapped when the tides receded. I never expected to find more than a few white conks, but there you were. At first, I thought you were dead. Your body was cold and your breathing shallow. I called for the others and then pulled you into my arms. I still remember when you first opened your eyes—and captured my heart."

Eramus remembered too. Inara's face was his earliest memory. She was different now; her skin had filled with wrinkles and her hair held long strands of silver between clumps of brown. Everything before that moment was a complete mystery. As a young child, fear had gripped him like a prisoner bound in chains. He had trusted no one but Inara those first few days. Her genuine compassion made him feel safe from the beginning, and he had refused to leave her side.

"I guessed you were not more than seven or eight. We tried for hours to get you to talk, but you didn't say a word. Arnan inquired around Olgetha, but no one recognized you. I refused to leave you. I couldn't bear to think of someone so young being left alone. It wasn't until our trip home that you finally told me your name. And when you fell asleep on my lap, I decided right there and then to take you in."

He sighed. His name was the only thing he could remember from his past. Occasionally, he would hear voices while he slept, but his mind could never conjure an image to accompany them. Eramus liked to imagine they were the remnants of people who cared about him, perhaps even still searched for their lost child. While he had no way to confirm such a thing, the idea always left a pleasant warmth in his chest.

"Was there anything else besides just...me?" he asked, although he already knew the answer. Inara had told him everything time and again, always the same. He hoped she had simply forgotten something, overlooked a minute detail that could provide insight.

"No, dear. It was just you and a great deal of debris. I could tell straight away that you had washed ashore after the storm. Shipwrecked, without a doubt. The storm was the worst I'd seen in years, so it made sense. Your survival was a miracle."

Eramus shook his head. "I don't believe it was a miracle at all." He held his hands out and concentrated. Blue light encircled them. It danced around his palms and flooded his arms with warmth. "I think my power saved me, but..."

His stomach knotted. His power could be dangerous, and in his youth, there were times he had lost control. What if the ship sank because of him? What if he was responsible? His past could be littered with countless deaths that were the result of his *gift*.

"Don't you do that."

Eramus lifted his gaze. Her accusing finger was directed at him again. "Don't you dare blame yourself. We don't know what happened. We may never know, but I refuse to believe it was your fault. You have always been compassionate and were the sweetest child I'd ever seen."

Eramus swallowed, attempting to moisten his dry throat. "You don't know what I was like before. *I* don't know what I was like. My powers could easily sink a ship if I lost control. There have been times it has happened in this very house."

Inara folded her arms. "Sure, but it was always harmless. Remember the time I asked you to help with the dishes? You thought you could use your gift to do the work for you. What a disaster that turned out to be!"

Eramus ran his fingers through his hair and laughed. "I didn't see any reason to work if I didn't need to, but cleaning up armfuls of bubbles is more difficult than simply scrubbing a plate. I learned a valuable lesson that day."

"Ah, so you did. You were a good boy. I worried about you for a long time. You were so afraid of the world—of yourself, even. A dark experience can have a negative effect on a child...and on adults, too. Sometimes memories can be so painful that we learn to block them out. We learn to pretend they never happened, but the scars can never be hidden. Even in our greatest attempts at concealment, our pasts shine through. They are, after all, what led us to the present."

"I wish my past *would* shine through. I want to know what happened, to know who I am and where my powers came from. Part of my life has always been a mystery, and I feel my soul will never rest until I can understand. Until I find myself."

Inara stood and walked around the table towards him. She leaned down and kissed the top of his head. "Someday you will, dear. And when you do, I will be right here to listen. Just know that no matter what you discover, you will always be my Eramus. You will always be my son."

Tears pricked his eyes. Eramus rose and wrapped his arms around her. "Thank you, Mother, for saving me in every way."

She pulled away, a wide smile on her face. "I am completely exhausted. I think I will go to bed. Sleep well, my dear." She patted his cheek. "And don't forget to shave in the morning."

Eramus chuckled and nodded. Inara left him alone in the darkening room, the only light emanating from the candle in the center of the table. He plopped down in the chair and placed his clasped hands against his forehead. He closed his eyes and focused on the memories of that day on the shore. The image of Inara's face, hovering over him on the sandy beach, flashed into his mind. He pinched his eyes tighter. If he could only discover the memories that lay just beyond his reach. They felt so close, and yet...

He opened his eyes and sighed. Someday he would find answers, even if it required a lifetime to do it.

* * *

The air was warm. Eramus chucked off the multicolored blanket and rolled over. He struggled to sleep when it was hot, and tonight was proving no different. Even when his heavy eyes closed, his mind couldn't rest. It wandered to the sea, where a massive wooden ship tossed in the waves. Blue light glowed between small cracks in the hull, causing the ship to swell under the force until it exploded into a storm of debris. He imagined himself as a small child at the center of the event, the lone survivor of the disaster. But nothing about those images seemed real. Not like his memories of Inara, when she had found him nearly dead on the beach.

Slowly, the images shifted to a stormy sea and a darkening sky. The ship creaked against the surging waves, tilting from side to side until it capsized. Screams sounded from all around him. A tight embrace held him close as he trembled. Water flooded the small cabin, and then he was in the open sea, fighting the waves with flailing limbs. He gasped before the turbulence pulled him under. His lungs burned, but he could find no air.

A flash of brilliant blue light surrounded him, and he breathed in the salty air. A soft voice filled his mind like a lullaby, singing him off to sleep.

"Take care, my love. We'll be together again soon."

CHAPTER FOUR
Motley Opinions

Water thundered over the large wooden wheel, thrusting it forward and causing the axle to spin. Eramus watched the pit wheel begin to turn, followed by the wallower and great spur. The entire mechanism was a marvel to him. Each piece worked in harmony with the others, all for the single purpose of grinding wheat. Even though his abilities allowed him to do what many considered the impossible, the ingenuity of man always impressed him. Grinding grain by hand required far more manpower and time than allowing the river to do the work for them.

He watched each of the cogs spin while he waited for Ordin to reach the third floor. The man's shadow moved across the upper level and stopped in front of the grain feeder. Ordin leaned over the rail and waved down to him. "All right!" he yelled over the roar of the waterwheel. "Send up the first sack!"

Eramus pulled hard on the rope that wrapped over a pulley, lifting a large sack of wheat into the air. The bag ascended higher with each tug until it reached the granary. Ordin gripped the burlap and guided it to the floor before untying the rope.

"Next sack!" he shouted, the sound muffled against the boom of the water.

Eramus tied another bag to the rope and pulled until the wheat reached Ordin's level. They repeated this process for nearly an hour, sending twenty sacks to the third floor.

"Give me a few minutes to get everything ready," said Ordin, cupping his hands to either side of his mouth so Eramus could hear him over the noise.

Eramus plopped down on the floor. His arms burned, and his chest heaved with each gasp. He could have easily lifted those sacks of grain with his magic, but how would Ordin have responded? Every villager he passed this morning on his way to the mill had given him suspicious looks. Some had even ducked inside their homes upon spotting him.

None of this came as a surprise. Eramus knew the people would fear his powers, and he couldn't blame them. Even he didn't know what he was fully capable of.

He leaned back, propping his body up with his arms. Ordin moved briskly across the upper level, positioning the sacks before they would begin grinding the wheat into flour. For the past two years, Eramus had worked as Ordin's apprentice. The man claimed three decades of expertise as a miller and garnered great respect from the community. This apprenticeship was an honorable position that would provide a comfortable future for Eramus.

But his actions had placed that in jeopardy. This morning, Ordin had greeted him in his usual cheerful manner, but Eramus could sense the emotions the man attempted to hide. His eyes held what appeared to be sympathy, but they left Eramus unsettled, and he couldn't shake the feeling that revealing his magic would have severe repercussions on his future livelihood. Perhaps he should use his power to help with their work? If the people saw him continually using it for good, they might be more accepting.

"Ready?" Ordin's dulled voice barely made it to Eramus's ears.

He stood and brushed the dirt from his brown trousers before climbing the stairs to the second floor. "Ready!" he called back, resolving to push the negative thoughts from his mind. He could speak to Ordin about his powers later. Right now, they had work to do.

Eramus positioned several casks near the millstones. Ordin filled the chute with grain, and in minutes, Eramus was scooping the fine powder into the cask. The process took several hours, and by the time they had ground all the grain, five barrels of flour rested beside him. Eramus began hauling them to the ground floor to a separate storage room while Ordin cleaned the upper level. They met outside when their tasks were completed.

Ordin stretched and released a lazy yawn. "Good work today." He flashed a soft smile, but the sadness in his tone left Eramus uneasy again.

"I enjoy working with you. You've taught me much these last two years. I can never thank you enough for the opportunity."

The man stared at the ground, kicking at the dirt with the tip of his black boot. "I've enjoyed having you." His pause made Eramus's stomach knot. It was folly to hope the people would forgive his deceit. His actions threatened to pull everything he'd worked for out from under him. Perhaps being forced to leave would have been the better outcome.

Ordin sighed. "With all that has happened, I think it might be best for you to take some time off from the mill. I'm sure that's not what you want to hear, but I believe it's for the best. Just until things calm down, of course."

"Of course. I understand."

"No, I don't think you do." Ordin rested his hand on Eramus's shoulder. He tilted his head and his bushy mustache twitched with the lift of his mouth. "I voted for you to stay. I want to keep you on as my apprentice, but the people need time to see, to understand. You're a good man—magic powers or not. They will all come around; I'm certain of it."

"I hope you are right. This village is my life. I don't want to think about leaving, but..." Eramus ran his fingers through his hair. He didn't know what he would do if it came to that. Where would he go? How could he ever leave Inara?

"I'll have another large load of wheat to do next week. I'll expect you back then." Ordin slapped his hand against Eramus's shoulder. "And I'll also expect you to use your gift to help with the work. I thought you might do so today, even." Ordin gave him a pointed look.

Eramus laughed. "I had contemplated asking, but the last thing I wanted to do was make you uncomfortable."

"Uncomfortable? No, what makes me uncomfortable is the way this old back aches after moving sacks of grain around all day. If magic can alleviate that, then I'm all for it." He jerked his chin towards the village. "I've got a few things left to do here, but you head on back. I'll see you next week."

Eramus nodded. "Thank you. I'll be here."

Walking through his village with eyes and whispers following him only added to the mixture of emotions fighting for control. He was grateful that Ordin had not cut him off completely, but Eramus had hoped work would provide a welcome distraction from the constant looks of disapproval. Now he faced them with nothing to free his mind from the trepidation weighing on him.

He turned the corner of a large stone cottage and nearly collided with a young boy and his mother. "Forgive me," he said, reaching out to steady the child.

The woman gripped the boy's shoulders and yanked him backwards with wide eyes. The fear they held made his heart sink. Eramus had spent a decade hiding his powers for this very reason. People were always afraid of the unknown, of things they didn't understand, and his power certainly fit those categories. No matter how much good he did with his gift, it might never be enough to convince them he had no desire to hurt anyone.

His shoulders slumped as he watched their two figures

disappear out of sight. People he'd known for years now treated him like a stranger, or worse, a criminal they couldn't trust. Eramus trudged to the edge of the clearing and sat down on the grass. He leaned against a thick oak and closed his eyes.

"You look exhausted."

Evree's voice startled him. He pushed himself from the ground so quickly he nearly toppled over. "Evree, I was just...how are you?"

She clasped her hands in front of her. "I'm well. Thank you, Eramus." Her smile made his stomach flutter. Evree stepped towards him and placed her hand on the rough bark of the oak tree. Her fingers dug into the grooves, and her eyes darted over the trunk as if she were studying every crevice. "How are you holding up?" she asked in an almost whisper.

Eramus chuckled and shook his head. "I believe I should ask you that. You went through quite the ordeal yesterday. How are you?"

She twisted her lavender colored skirt between her fingers and looked down at the ground, allowing strands of golden blonde hair to fall around her face. "You did ask me. Twice now." A flood of warmth rushed to his face when she giggled. "But I'm perfectly fine, thanks to you."

He swallowed and rubbed his hands against his trousers. They were sweaty. Why were his hands so sweaty? "I'm just glad you are all right. And your father, how is he?"

"Safe and sound." She took a step towards him and his heart galloped. "Again, I have you to thank for that."

"You don't need to thank me. I want no harm to befall you or anyone in the village."

She lifted lone shoulder. "Well, I suppose you will just have to deal with my gratitude. My father and I both wish to offer it. He's asked me to invite you to dinner."

For a moment, he could only blink at her. Was this conversation truly happening? Minutes ago he was being completely avoided, and now, Evree had invited him to dinner. Perhaps if he pinched himself hard enough, he would wake up.

He winced, but Evree remained in front of him.

"Unless you don't want to come to dinner?"

Heat spread through his face again. Eramus stepped forward, leaving only a few feet between them. "Yes, of course! I'm honored you would ask me to come to dinner. Please, forgive my hesitation. The offer merely took me by surprise."

"And why is that?"

"I..." Eramus kicked at the ground and sighed. "The revelation of my power has incited various reactions. How can I expect anyone to trust something even I don't comprehend?"

Evree placed her hand on his arm, and the sensation sent chills through his body. A set of warm green eyes stared up at him, easing the tightness in his chest. "You saved me, Eramus. How could I have any doubt about your character after that? Your ability doesn't change who you are. No matter what, you are Eramus, a good and honorable man."

He couldn't help but smile. Not all of his people shared Evree's opinion, but it was hers that he valued most. That she thought no less of him because of the magic he possessed was more than he had dared to hope for.

"Thank you. You don't know how much your words mean to me."

Evree bunched her skirts between her fingers, lifting them from the ground just enough to reveal a pair of brown boots. "I will see you soon, then. At sunset?"

Eramus nodded. "Sunset."

His eyes followed her as she flitted away, her lavender gown barely grazing the ground and her gait smooth as though she walked on air.

She'd invited him to dinner.

The excitement made his heart do strange things. Eramus glanced up at the sky. The sun was well on its way to descending behind the mountains in the distance. Sunset couldn't be more than an hour away.

Blast.

He examined the state of his clothes, wincing as he brushed the dirt from his shoulder. He would need a bath before going to dinner. Fine flour had a way of filling into every fold and crack it could find. Even his hair typically had wisps of white after working in the mill all morning. His appearance likely displayed a wretched state.

As he made his way back through the village, he didn't notice the stares and whispers. His heart raced with anticipation and his mind recanted Evree's words. She'd said he was an honorable man. Perhaps Ordin was right to think that the people would eventually see him for the respectable man he strived to be. Kieran and Evree had not lingered on the event other than to offer him gratitude with an invitation to dine with them. Maybe, in time, others would accept his gift as well.

Eramus drew in a deep breath as he entered his cottage. Tonight he would spend time with Evree, but he also hoped to make a good impression on Kieran as well. If he stood any chance of courting the man's daughter, this dinner would have to go well.

"There's nothing to worry about," he mumbled to himself as he pulled his dirty brown tunic over his head. "Kieran and I have always got on well enough."

Worrying would only make him more anxious. Kieran had invited *him*. That must mean something, after all.

CHAPTER FIVE
Dinner Impressions

"It's only dinner, Mother."

Eramus rolled his eyes as Inara made another lap around him. She'd already completed several turns, analyzing every aspect of his appearance and even swept a few locks of his black hair to one side.

"Of course it is," she muttered, encircling him again.

"Then why are we acting like I'll be in the presence of royalty?"

Inara stopped in front of him, her hands planted firmly on her hips. "If you don't think highly enough of Evree to present yourself with decency, then you don't deserve her."

Eramus grimaced. "That's not...you know I do, but I don't think she's going to care if my shirt isn't perfectly—"

"Good impressions are key to gaining a father's approval for courtship."

He groaned. She was right, but that didn't mean he intended to admit it. Eramus wanted to court Evree, but after the way the villagers had responded to the revelation of his magic, he wasn't sure courting anyone was an option.

"Look at your trousers! What a mess! You've got dirt"—she bent forward and brushed the barely visible patch from his black pants—"everywhere."

Eramus slapped her hand away. "Honestly, Mother. I think I've grown enough to brush the dirt from my own trousers."

She folded her arms. "Then don't stand there like you're incapable and get on with it." She rushed to the other side of the cottage, muttering as she mindlessly placed a few dishes into her wash basin. "Grown. Yet he asked for *my* help."

Eramus chuckled and shook his head. He hadn't asked for help; he'd inquired about how he *looked*. The mistake was asking anything at all. His mother was nearly as anxious as him, although he knew she had meant well by her slight at his poor attempt to look presentable.

He brushed the small bit of dirt from his pants and drew in a deep breath. "All right. Time to go."

She rushed back to his side, a wide grin on her face. "Oh, you look so handsome! Just remember to be yourself...and don't say anything stupid...and be charming, but not too char—"

"I think that's enough advice for the moment," he said, taking her hand. She was only making him more nervous at this point. "I'll be fine."

"You're my son; how could you not be?" She patted his cheek, and a deep scowl filled in her wrinkle lines. "You didn't shave."

Eramus rubbed his fingers across his prickly skin. With his thoughts running amok, he'd forgotten about tending to his stubble this morning. "I suppose I could—"

"No, no! There's no time for that now." Her hands pushed against his back, ushering him towards the door. "You mustn't be late. That's poor manners, and I won't have anyone thinking I didn't raise you properly."

Blotches of orange streaked the sky above, and the air had already cooled. He walked several yards before the soft thud of his cottage door reached his ears. Eramus imagined his mother watching him from the small window above the dining table, likely bouncing on her toes with excitement. She would demand a full report upon his return.

His heart raced as he neared Evree's cottage. He paused outside the door, his fist hovering in mid-air while he built up the courage to knock. When the door swung open, it wasn't Evree's bright smile that greeted him, but Kieran's stern eyes. The man's expression crumpled with confusion

"Eramus? What are you doing here?"

His heart stopped. Kieran didn't know why he was here? His face must have reflected his own confusion, because Kieran's brows lifted to his hairline. Eramus cleared his throat. "Dinner...Evree invited me."

Kieran's shoulders slumped, and he growled as he turned away.

"Evree!"

Her golden hair bounced against her face as she skipped towards them, undaunted by her father's folded arms and pinched brows. "Eramus! I'm so glad you're here!"

"You invited him to dinner...*without* my permission?" Kieran's eyes darted between the two of them before lingering on him, but unlike Evree, Eramus fidgeted under the man's icy stare.

Evree shrugged. "Yes."

Kieran had no time to respond. Evree grabbed Eramus by the wrist and yanked him inside. He stumbled and clutched the wall to stop himself from fumbling to the floor. What was she thinking? Inviting him without her father's approval? Would Kieran assume he played a role in this? Eramus swallowed. They had yet to sit down at the table and already tonight was a disaster.

"Dinner is almost ready, if the two of you would take a seat." Evree gestured towards the square table on the east side of the room and smiled. "I'll just be a minute or two."

She whirled around and flitted away, leaving the two of them alone by the door. Eramus turned to Kieran, whose face was as firm as stone. "I...Kieran, if I had known—"

Kieran lifted his hand to stop him. "Don't worry yourself over it. Evree is spirited, just like her mother was. When she wants something, she doesn't hesitate to go after it."

Eramus tilted his head. "Wants something?"

The man's firm expression cracked into a small grin as he chuckled. He offered no response to the question, instead moving across the room to sit down.

Wants something? What did he mean by that? Surely Evree didn't want...

Eramus pushed the thought away. He could not linger on that right now. Evree had invited him without her father's knowledge, and her actions put him in a difficult position. He'd arrived believing he was welcome in their home, but now he wasn't so sure. Kieran seemed to accept the situation, but that was not the same as approval.

He joined Kieran at the table, and the two of them sat in silence. Eramus searched his befuddled thoughts for something to say. He found no success in the endeavor, and relief flooded over him when Evree glided into the room and placed trays of food before them. She sat down, her demeanor as cheerful as ever.

"I'm happy you could dine with us tonight, Eramus," she said, flashing him a smile that made his stomach flutter.

He needed to respond but had no idea what to say. He was happy Evree had invited him, but he couldn't express that with Kieran scowling right next to him at the end of the table. Eramus had yet to determine whether his presence angered the man, or if he merely found him inconvenient.

"I appreciate the offer," he said, avoiding Kieran's gaze. Hopefully, those few words would suffice.

"It's the least we could do," she continued, and Eramus thought his pounding heart might kill him before the meal was through. "You saved us both from injury, if not something worse. The village should honor you for what you did. Wouldn't you agree, Papa?"

Eramus chewed the inside of his cheek and lifted his gaze just enough to glimpse Kieran's expression. His dark eyes pinned Eramus in place. "Is that what you want? To be honored for your heroism?"

"No," Eramus answered. "No, sir. I don't wish for honor or praise. That isn't why I saved you."

"Then why did you do it?"

Eramus turned to face Kieran fully. Did the man believe he had only acted because he would be revered? That certainly wasn't how things turned out, nor was it the reason he had revealed his power. The notion made Eramus's blood boil.

"Because it was the right thing to do!"

His chest heaved with his heavy breathing. Kieran's stoic expression remained unchanged. What was he thinking? He'd allowed Kieran to get under his skin. But he shouldn't have to defend his actions, especially when they had saved two people from harm.

Kieran sighed. "Forgive me, Eramus. I did not wish to sound accusatory. You are a good man and I am grateful for your willingness to help both me and my daughter in our time of need. I imagine your actions have already caused you to suffer, and I am sorry that you must endure hostility from our people. You do not deserve that."

The pounding in his chest eased. "I appreciate that, but I also understand their concerns. My power...not having a clear understanding of it worries me. I wish I knew more about myself so that I might alleviate their reservations and my own."

"Inara always said you couldn't remember anything about your past," said Kieran, curiosity filling his tone. "Is there nothing from before you came to the village that you can recall? No family or details of where you came from?"

Eramus shook his head. "No. I'm afraid I can't remember anything before the day she found me on the beach. Sometimes there are voices, like distant memories attempting to break the surface, but I can't seem to connect them with whom they belong."

Evree placed her hand on her chest, her green eyes full of sympathy as they reflected the flickering light of the candle in the center of the table. "I can't imagine how scary that must have been. A child, all alone without even memories of who they are..." Her voice trailed off and several moments of silence ensued.

"Well," said Kieran, wiping his mouth with a piece of cloth. "Regardless of where you came from, I am grateful you are here. If there is anything I can do to repay you, name it."

Eramus hesitated for a moment. He had never expected payment of any sort; he still didn't, but there was one thing he wanted—to court the man's daughter. Now, however, probably wasn't the best time to ask. Kieran was a hard man to read, and Eramus would need to spend more time in his presence before making his request. Rushing into this might ruin his only chance.

"I don't expect any sort of payment. I'm just glad that you are both safe."

Kieran's intense study left Eramus fidgeting in the chair. For a moment, Eramus had believed he won the man over, or at least made progress, but that stern expression could make even the sun question its reason for existence.

"It's growing late," said Kieran as he rose. Eramus and Evree stood, too, just as Kieran cleared his throat. "Thank you for joining us."

Evree bounded around the table to stand beside him. "May I walk you out?"

Eramus glanced at Kieran, hoping to decipher the man's opinion before answering her. The man unfolded his arms and swatted the air. "Go on. She wouldn't listen if I said no, anyway. Just don't give me any reason to chase you off."

Eramus swallowed hard. It wasn't the most reassuring response, but indifference was better than a flat *no*. Evree wrapped her hand around his arm, and his heart picked up speed. When they passed through the cottage door, moonlight illuminated her face. His breath caught.

"Thank you for coming." Her chin dipped towards the ground and she twisted a strand of her long blonde hair between her fingers. "I'm sorry I lied to you about Papa. I was afraid you wouldn't come if you knew it had been my invitation alone."

"Your assumption would have been correct."

Evree bit her lip, avoiding his gaze. Her disappointment made him smile. There was something endearing about that furrowed forehead. "My objection would not have come from a lack of desire to spend time with you," he continued. "But because I prefer your father to hold me in high regard. Gaining his approval would be difficult if he thought me anything but an honorable man. It already will be, considering recent events."

"Gaining his approval for what?"

She stared up at him, searching his expression, but the slight tug of her lips suggested she already knew the answer. Eramus wasn't sure if that made him more nervous or less. He rubbed the back of his neck with his hand, his skin burning.

He searched for the right words. To court her? To call on her? Was that moving too fast? After all, other than acting like a fool in her presence, he had shown no inclination that he was interested...at least he hadn't meant to. His mother seemed to believe his affection was obvious.

"I'd like to get to know you better," he said, finally settling on something more vague. He wasn't ready for a total confession. Not yet.

Evree's smile grew. "You know, I often enjoy spending time in the meadow in the mornings. It's a beautiful place, peaceful. The only downside is that sometimes I get rather lonely not having anyone to enjoy it with."

Was that an invitation? Judging by the coyness in her expression, he concluded it must be. "I see. Perhaps tomorrow you won't find yourself alone in the meadow?"

She stepped closer, eliminating nearly all the space between them. "Perhaps I won't."

His heart stopped, and his gaze fell to her lips. What would it be like to brush his own against them? He'd imagined kissing Evree before, but with her standing so close and the glimmer of moonlight reflecting off her skin...

The cottage door flew open and smacked against the interior wall with a loud bang. Kieran stood in the doorframe, his arms folded and his face pinched. "Time to come inside, Evree."

She giggled. "Yes, Papa."

Before Eramus could react, she lifted on her toes and planted a soft kiss on his cheek. Heat rushed over his entire face, and for a moment, he froze in place. Her call from the door released him. "Goodnight, Eramus."

He opened his mouth to respond, but nothing came out. Her giggles became muffled as she disappeared from view. Kieran's dark eyes glared at him. Realizing his mouth still hung open, he snapped it closed.

Kieran growled. "You're making me regret standing against Arnan, but I suppose that's not entirely your fault." Kieran pointed at him. "Do right by my daughter or no amount of magic will save you. Is that clear?"

"Yes, sir." It was all Eramus could manage.

The cottage door closed with a soft thud, and Eramus breathed a sigh of relief. None of *that* had gone how he expected, but somehow he still felt he had made progress. Other than the threat, Kieran had all but given him permission to see his daughter.

Eramus smiled as he walked home under the light of the moon. He touched where Evree's warm kiss still lingered on his skin. The meadow—he would see her there tomorrow, and already his heart danced with excitement.

CHAPTER SIX
The Stranger in the Black Cloak

The air held the sweet aroma of flowers. A myriad of colors dotted the garden beds to either side of the stone path. Eramus glided his palm along a dark green hedge, and the leaves tickled the tips of his fingers. He passed several statues of birds with outstretched wings, their fierce gazes staring down at him as if he were prey. The intensity in their marble eyes made him shudder.

Somehow, the scene before him looked familiar—*felt* familiar—like a long lost memory. Was he dreaming?

Muffled voices sounded from the other side of the hedge,

growing louder as footsteps approached the arch just a few yards in front of him. His eyes lingered on the space between the vine-covered stones until three burly men appeared. Their boisterous laughter made his stomach knot.

They passed through the structure and halted upon spotting him. One, whose red hair glistened with sweat, stared down at him with a malicious smirk. "Well, look what we have here! Little Eramus."

Eramus took a step back, his instincts screaming for him to run. But why? Who were these men, and why were their faces familiar?

"Careful, Whitmer," said another, placing his hand on the sheathed sword at his side. "You don't want to mess with the little devil. Might curse us."

Eramus balled his fists as the man's snicker echoed around him. Whitmer swatted the air. "What's he going to do? Even if he had magic, he's probably just like his old man—a coward. Look at his eyes. He's too terrified to even speak."

Whitmer lunged forward in mock assault. Eramus tripped over his own feet and stumbled to the ground. All three men laughed. "You see!" said Whitmer. "What did I tell you? Just like his father."

Eramus pushed himself from the stone pavers. "My father is not a coward!"

"Hah! Is that why he left you and your mother here?" Whitmer took three steps towards him, and his wide shadow encompassed Eramus. "He's a coward and a traitor. And you'll end up just like him."

The sensation that flowed through his veins was one he

recognized. The familiar warmth spread throughout his body, but he held in the desire to unleash it. "He left to save us," he whispered. "You could never understand. He wasn't a coward or a traitor!"

"He abandoned you," said Whitmer. "Been hiding for eight years."

"That's not true!"

"He's afraid. Disgraced. He knows he can't show his face here."

Bright blue light surrounded Eramus's body and flowed away from him in all directions. All of his bottled emotion exploded with his power, and the energy wave sent Whitmer and the others flying backwards. Three bodies landed on the garden walkway.

Panic overtook him. Eramus launched forward, running as fast as his legs could carry him. He rounded a corner and crashed into something solid. Fingers gripped around his upper arms. Eramus stared up into dark, stern eyes. The jewels that adorned the man's elegant attire glistened in the sunlight.

"How long?"

Eramus jerked, attempting to dislodge the grip that held him in place. The man pulled him in close and tilted his head so that he was level with Eramus's face. "How long have you had magic?"

When Eramus remained silent, a wide grin stretched over the man's lips. "Come now, Eramus. You can tell your uncle. It will be our little secret."

His sinister laugh filled Eramus's ears. The man's body disintegrated into a swirl of black dust.

Eramus gasped, shooting upright in bed. His eyes darted over the familiar objects of his room enveloped in shadow. The nightmare had ended, but his breathing remained ragged. His shirt stuck to his sticky skin and beads of sweat rolled down his forehead.

What was all of that? Were those images...real?

Eramus weaved his fingers through his hair. He had no recollection of those men, but his gut told him he had once known them. Somewhere, deep in the corners of his mind, his memories waited to resurface, and tonight, one of them had. But what did it mean? Those men had accused his father of being a traitor. For all Eramus knew, it was the truth. And what of the other man, the one with the dark eyes and expensive clothing? His uncle?

He had always wanted to remember his past, but this small glimpse only left him with more questions, more frustration.

A smidgen of sunlight pierced through the shadows near his window. Eramus tugged on each of his leather boots and watched the sky illuminate, the black, starry curtain vanishing to reveal a shade of bright blue.

He devoured a slice of bread and a dark red apple. Evree had said she would go to the meadow this morning, but he didn't know how early she would make the short walk to the grassy field outside their village. The sooner he could leave the cottage, the better, even if it meant waiting. He'd wait all day to spend even a few minutes in her company.

With nothing left of his meal but crumbs, Eramus marched towards the door.

"Where are you going so early?"

Blast.

He forced a cheerful smile and turned. Inara stood on the

opposite side of the room, her arms folded and her brows raised.

"Good morning, Mother. I trust you slept well?"

Her eyes narrowed. "Don't change the subject. Where are you going...and why are you being so secretive about it?"

"I thought a walk and some fresh air might serve me well. I was going to the meadow. Wanted to clear my head."

He chewed the inside of his cheek. Lying to Inara made his stomach churn. But he wasn't really lying, just leaving out a few details. Last night, she had demanded to know everything that happened at dinner. Of course, he hadn't *actually* told her everything. Not about the meadow or the soft kiss Evree placed on his cheek.

Her exuberance had unnerved him all the same, and when she mentioned wedding decorations...

A shiver spread through his body. No, she needn't know he planned to see Evree.

Inara drummed her fingers against her arm. "All right. I suppose you must have a great deal on your mind. Would you like me to come with you?"

"No!"

The word came out with more force than he intended. Inara's expression broke, her lips curling up on one side and a glint in her eyes that sparkled with mischief. "Very well. Be careful, then."

She moseyed over to the washbasin and set to work on some dishes. Even from across the room, he could see the grin still plastered on her face. She couldn't possibly know, could she?

Eramus rubbed the back of his neck. "I'll see you later, Mother."

"Goodbye, dear." She didn't so much as glance at him, but he could still hear the amusement in her tone.

Inara knew. Or at minimum, suspected.

The village rested quietly in the early hours of morning. He passed two people along the main path, and both offered him a polite, albeit reserved, smile. It would take time to earn back the trust he had lost, but there was hope. He turned the corner of a large cottage with a red thatched roof, picking up his pace. The last person he desired to see was—

"Eramus."

Arnan's deep baritone fell over him, halting his steps. If there was one person who could kill his excitement this morning, it was the man standing behind him. Eramus turned and cleared his throat.

"Good morning, Arnan."

The man folded his arms and studied him for a moment. "Where are you going?"

The demand irked Eramus, but he forced himself to remain calm. If he wanted to earn back the trust of his people, he would have to endure Arnan's prejudice. "I'm taking a walk to the meadow."

"Why?"

Eramus clenched his jaw. "Because it's a lovely day."

Arnan narrowed his eyes and stepped closer. He jabbed his finger at Eramus's chest. "Just because the vote allowed you to stay doesn't mean you're wanted here. This *power* of yours is a threat to us all, and when the others finally see it, they'll demand your banishment. One misstep...that's all I need to convince them."

Eramus wanted nothing more than to rebuff, to defend himself, but it would do no good to argue. Arnan wanted him gone, and any mistake would give the man leverage.

Arnan backed away and sneered before entering his cottage. Eramus released a heavy breath. His life felt like a sea of broken glass, and he was a ship maneuvering through the shards. It was only a matter of time before one cut so deep that he would plummet into the dark depths below.

Tiny yellow and purple flowers dotted the meadow. The dark green grass stretched for a hundred yards before meeting a thick forest of oak and pine. Eramus closed his eyes, listening to the chirping of the blue jays that fluttered between the trees. Evree was right; the meadow was peaceful.

"You came."

Eramus turned around. Evree's pale pink dress was a sharp contrast against the grassy meadow. She fit perfectly with the scene of pretty flowers, and her smile could easily outdo the warmth of the sun. He tilted his head and faked a scowl. "You doubted I would come?"

She averted her eyes. "I thought my father might have scared you off after last night."

"He left me with a threat, but nothing I would consider more than fatherly protectiveness." He stepped closer to her. "And nothing that would scare me away."

"I'm relieved to hear that."

She gathered her skirts and plopped down on the ground.

Eramus sat down beside her. For several minutes, they were both quiet, then Evree took his hand and traced the lines in his palms. He forgot how to breathe.

"What does your power feel like?" she asked.

Her touch had his thoughts so befuddled it took him several seconds to form words. "Warm. It feels...warm." Much in the way he felt right now.

"Would you show me?"

Eramus hesitated. He didn't want to scare her, but her soft expression eased his concerns. He pulled his hand away and focused until an orb of blue light hovered above his palm.

Evree gasped. "It's beautiful!"

She leaned in closer and the light reflected off her face. Evree wasn't afraid of his magic, her reaction more one of fascination. He smiled and pushed the orb into the air. They both watched it ascend until the light dispersed into the sky.

"Amazing," she whispered.

Eramus stared down at the ground, his forehead furrowed. "Not everyone believes so."

Evree shrugged. "You should not care what everyone thinks."

"Perhaps, but this is a complicated situation. They almost forced me to leave. This is my home. I don't want to lose it or the people I care about."

"Am I on that list? Of people you care about?"

Heat flooded his face. "I think you know you are."

She bit her lip and scooted closer, her shoulder brushing against his. "I'm glad that I am."

For several hours, Eramus enjoyed her company. They discussed everything from his powers to the way Roderick cursed when his neighbor's sheep ate his flowers. With time, his pounding heart eased, and their shared laughter made him forget his concerns.

Evree plucked a small white flower from the ground and held it in front of her face. She studied it for a moment before pulling it close to her nose. Seconds later, her dainty sneeze made him chuckle.

"Oh, dear," she said, rubbing her watery eyes. "I should know better than to sniff the flowers. They always make me sneeze, but I admire them so much that I can't break the habit."

Eramus took the white flower from her hand and twirled it between his fingers. "Which ones are your favorite?"

"I quite like the clovers, but I believe daisies are my favorite."

He made a mental note. One day, he would surprise her with a full bouquet of daisies. Perhaps flowers were the key to earning more kisses. He'd bring her a bouquet everyday if it meant—

"Which one is your favorite?"

"What?"

She giggled. "Flowers? I was wondering which was your favorite."

His favorite? Eramus ran his fingers through his hair. He'd never really given flowers much thought, let alone taken a fancy to any kind in particular. His eyes bounced between her and the meadow. "The yellow ones."

"Buttercups? A wonderful choice. They are lovely, aren't they?"

She plucked one from the ground and handed it to him.

Lovely. He supposed they were, but he chose them because the bright yellow reminded him of Evree. Golden hair and a warm smile—nothing could be lovelier than that.

Evree glanced up at the clouds and sighed. "It's nearly noon. I told Papa I would be back by then." Her lips pursed into a pout. "I wish I could stay."

Eramus shook his head. "I don't want your father upset with me."

"Will I see you here tomorrow? Promise me I will."

Eramus chuckled. "I promise; I'll be here."

He stood and assisted Evree from the ground. He had half a mind to walk her back to the village, but Eramus wasn't sure the people or Kieran would respond well to that.

"I think I'll stay here for a while," he said. "I've always had to hide my magic, but now that everyone knows, I can use it without fear someone will see. It might sound strange, but I wouldn't mind the opportunity to practice."

"Practice. And then I expect you to show me more tomorrow."

"You have a deal, Miss Evree." Eramus held out his hand, and she shook it, a wide grin spreading across her face.

She darted forward and pressed her lips against his cheek, taking him by surprise again. "Goodbye, Eramus." She held her skirts as she strolled away. Eramus placed his palm against his face. He could get used to those kisses.

Eramus whirled his hands through the air, conjuring orbs of light and clouds of magical dust. Practicing in the open was an incredible freedom he'd never experienced. He'd never felt more himself, and after spending the entire morning with Evree, his power was stronger than usual. Eramus had noted that his emotions affected the strength of his magic, especially when he was happy or angry.

He willed the blue energy to surround a long fallen tree. Eramus lifted it into the air and sat it down several yards away.

"Impressive."

The unfamiliar voice sent shivers down his spine. He spun around. A man dressed in a long, black cloak stood before him, his mouth contorted into a crooked smile.

"Who are you?" asked Eramus. Something about the man unnerved him, or perhaps it was the fact that a stranger had witnessed his magic. Either way, Eramus's insides twisted.

The man chuckled, as if Eramus's reaction amused him. "For now, you may think of me as a friend, Eramus. I'm here to help you."

CHAPTER SEVEN
Hidden Gems

His hair hung over his shoulders with a few pieces tied at the back of his head. Red streaks the color of blood weaved between jet black locks, and his dark eyes popped in contrast with his pale white skin. Small wrinkles on his forehead and near the corners of his eyes suggested he was much older than Eramus, but his tight sleeves revealed a person in top physical condition.

Eramus's stomach twisted. The man's sudden appearance and demeanor made his heart race. "What do you mean, you are here to help?"

"Just that," replied the stranger. "I know the power you possess, and I can teach you how to use it, how to control your magical energies. You don't know your full potential, Eramus."

"And you do? You don't know me, so how could you possibly understand?"

The man chuckled. "A question with a simple answer. I understand because I am like you. I know what it's like for magic to flow through your veins, for it to be fueled by your emotions—a caged animal waiting to be unleashed."

"You can wield magic?"

Eramus narrowed his eyes. The only known occurrence of magic he was aware of came from the rumored battle between the previous king of Izarden and a powerful sorcerer. It was said that every soldier found death that day, including King Sytal, leaving his son to inherit the throne. The new king insisted his father had gone to face a magic wielder, a man who had once held a top rank in Izarden's army. But there was no proof the battle that had decimated the militia was against a sorcerer. King Sytal had led Izarden into many conflicts with neighboring kingdoms, and any of them could have sought revenge.

"I will not take the word of a stranger just like that," said Eramus. "Prove it to me. If you can use magic, show me now."

The man's expression tightened. "I suppose I must correct my statement. I was *once* like you. My ability to use magic is...gone. At least for the time being."

"Gone?"

Eramus chewed the inside of his cheek. Could a person lose their ability to use magic? He had no way of knowing whether this stranger spoke the truth. It wasn't as though he knew other people like him. Even if there were more with similar powers, they probably kept them a secret, as he had done for the last decade.

The man released a heavy sigh. "Yes, gone. Other wielders stole my power from me years ago. But that is not what is important right now. You wished for proof, and I can attempt to provide it for you."

He reached inside his cloak and pulled a small, jagged dagger from inside. Eramus took a step back, and the man held up his hand. "I've no desire to hurt you, Eramus. I am a friend who only wants to help."

Eramus's gaze fell to the dagger. He'd never seen anything quite like it. The jagged blade glistened in the sunlight, but it was the blue gemstone in the hilt that captured his attention.

"A young man forged this dagger with magic." He flipped the piece so that the handle pointed towards Eramus. "The gemstone you see here is...well, let's just say it's very rare. The same magic that flows through your veins exists inside this stone. It is part of what little magic I still have control over. I hope it will be enough to ease your concerns."

The gemstone illuminated, and a faint blue aura surrounded the hilt. Eramus could sense the magical energy as it glowed. Whether he could trust the man or not, Eramus knew the stone contained a power similar to his own. He could feel it, like a pulsating wave that beckoned to him.

Eramus opened his mouth to speak, but words escaped him. He had so many questions, all fighting for priority. The man placed the dagger back inside his cloak and smiled. "I know you must have a thousand questions."

"And then some," said Eramus, scratching the back of his head. "I've never met anyone who didn't quake at the mention of magic, let alone who could use it."

The man laughed and gestured to the edge of the meadow where the tall oaks shaded the grassy ground below. "Perhaps we should move out of the sun first?"

Eramus nodded and followed him to the tree line. He remained uneasy about the situation, but curiosity fueled him forward. He may not trust this man in the black cloak, but he was desperate for answers. If he could understand more about his power and where it came from, perhaps his people would trust him again.

The man plopped down beside the oak and leaned against the bark. Eramus joined him, resting against a tree a few feet away. "Where shall we begin?" the man asked.

Eramus thought for a moment. Where did he want to begin? The man's name would be good to know, but too many other questions demanded answers. It was hard to know what to ask first, but he finally settled on what he thought was most important. "Are there others like me? More people who can wield magic?"

"As of now, there are six people in all of Virgamor with such power, including yourself."

"Six? And do you know them?"

The man's deep growl sent shivers down Eramus's spine. "In some ways, it is unfortunate that I do." He shifted on the grass and stared out into the meadow. Eramus wondered what the man was thinking with his intense gaze and tightly pinched brows. Did he have an unpleasant experience with other magic wielders? He said some of them had stolen his power, but why? And how?

Eramus plucked several blades of grass in frustration. This stranger was testing his patience.

"Perhaps it would be best if we started from the beginning," the man said, finally breaking his focus. "Magic, or at least its presence among humankind, has only existed for a few millennia. How much of Izarden's history do you know?"

Eramus shook his head. "Only a little. I live in an isolated village. We miss out on a great deal of news."

The man nodded. "I understand what that is like, but you should be grateful. The world can be a rather unforgiving place." His eyes glazed, but he continued, "About thirty years ago, mercenaries invaded our kingdom. They burned countless villages and slaughtered hundreds, never leaving survivors. Three children escaped from their grasps after these invaders destroyed their village, but rather than wallow in self pity, they set out in search of a weapon that could put an end to the destruction.

"They journeyed to what is now the kingdom of Selvenor. Deep in the mountains of Aknar, hidden away in a mysterious cavern, the Virgàm waited to be found."

"The Virgàm?" asked Eramus.

"A weapon. An enchanted scepter with four gemstones, just like the one embedded in my dagger. It is the source of magic in humans."

Source of magic? Eramus struggled to wrap his head around the notion. "How can this weapon be our source of magic? I don't understand. And where did it come from in the first place?"

He glared at the ground. For every question the man answered, ten more took its place.

"Long ago, a man who lived alone on Mt. Kantinar created the Virgàm. He witnessed a strange rock descend from the heavens, and upon studying it, found the piece filled with colorful stones. He could sense the power they contained and eventually created a vessel to hold them. The three children found the Virgàm, and when they touched the scepter, it granted them the ability to use magic. Your power comes directly from those four gems, passed on to you at birth."

Eramus's pulse quickened. Passed to him at birth? This man...could he know who his parents are? With so few magic wielders in the world, he probably did. Perhaps they even had a hand in him losing his power. The thought made Eramus shudder.

"So, these children gained the ability to use magic? What happened after that? Did they face the mercenaries?"

The man swiped a strand of black hair from his face. "They did, and they saved many lives. They obliterated the invaders, and the king honored them for their service to Izarden. Eventually, they had children of their own, passing on their abilities to a new generation." He nodded towards Eramus and smiled. "You."

Eramus swallowed hard. "I...you're saying one of my parents was a child from your story?"

"Yes, Eramus. That is what I'm saying." The man scooted closer to him and placed his hand firmly on Eramus's shoulder. "You don't know how strong you are, but I want to help you. I can teach you how to use your powers, if that is what you want?"

"I do. But..." Eramus ran his fingers through his hair. He wanted to control his magic, but what he wanted more was to understand his past. What had happened to his parents? And when did the images that haunted him come into play? He felt so close to having the answers he'd wanted for so long.

"I want to learn more about my power, but I also want to know who I am. Do you know about my family? What happened to them?"

The man sighed and stared at the ground, seeming reluctant to answer. "I know what happened to them, but I think that is a discussion for another day. I do not wish to overwhelm you, Eramus. Besides, I cannot stay. There are things I need to attend to."

Eramus's forehead furrowed. "You're leaving?"

"For now. But I will return in one week. I intend to train you, teach you everything I know about magic." He rose and brushed the grass from his dark trousers. "Meet me here. I promise I will tell you more then."

He slipped his hand inside his cloak, and for a moment, Eramus believed he would pull out the jagged dagger again. This time, however, the man held a round amulet in his palm. Silver metal twisted together in an intricate lattice, and a large, blue gem rested in the center.

"Another gem," he said, noting Eramus's confusion. "Hidden within the same cavern as the scepter were several of these gemstones. When the children grew older, they returned and took the precious stones back to Izarden. A second generation magic user forged several items, embedding the stones within them. In time, we learned each piece had its own unique ability." He held up the amulet and sunlight poured through the transparent stone, casting a shimmering blue reflection on the man's face. "This, for instance, can transport a person anywhere. One only needs to have been there previously for it to work."

Eramus stood and leaned against the thick trunk of the oak behind him. "So, you've been here before? How long have you known I could wield magic?"

"I've watched you for some time. I didn't want to approach you until I believed you were ready. Now that the village knows your secret, I thought it best you learned the truth. Trust is not a battle easily won, especially when you differ from those whose approval you seek."

Eramus couldn't disagree with that. Many of the people he'd known for years had now taken to avoiding him. But as much as he wanted to trust the man before him, the only person to provide long awaited answers, something about him prompted concern. This stranger held hostage the information Eramus desired, and for what reason, he didn't know. He couldn't help but question the man's motives.

"One week," the man said, stroking the amulet with his thumb. "I'll see you then."

"I have one last question for today," said Eramus. "I want to know your name."

A smile tugged at one side of the man's mouth. His body slowly disintegrated, swirling into a cloud of black dust. When all that remained was his head and shoulders, he whispered his response.

"My name is Morzaun."

CHAPTER EIGHT
Meetings of Magic

Eramus entered the mill, the sound of the cranking waterwheel soothing his soul. Something about the familiar noise set his mind at ease, despite how anxious he was to visit the meadow. He and Evree had met there every day for the last week, but today's meeting would be with someone else entirely.

Morzaun—the mysterious man in the black cloak.

Eramus still wasn't certain he trusted him. The man seemed eager to teach him about magic and how to control his power, but people often offered assistance as a facade for their own selfish purposes.

A shadowed figure moved along the top floor. Ordin

maneuvered down the ladder and jumped off a few feet from the bottom floor. Fine white dust covered his clothes, and sweat beaded on his forehead.

Eramus offered a warm smile, but the one Ordin returned was small and half-hearted. That wasn't good.

"Good morning, Ordin," he said, hoping he'd only imagined the lack of cheerfulness.

Ordin averted his gaze. "Hello, Eramus. I hope you are well?"

He'd be better if the man wasn't acting so unfriendly. "I'm fine. Are you well?"

Ordin finally looked up, his eyes full of sadness. The man had instructed him to return in one week to work the mill. Although the opportunity had allowed Eramus to spend time with Evree, the villagers' attitudes towards him had not changed, and Ordin could retract his plan to keep him on as his apprentice. Eramus's stomach flipped.

Ordin's shoulders slumped to accompany his heavy sigh. "I respect you too much not to be honest, Eramus. I know I said you would still have a place as my apprentice, but..." He closed his eyes and massaged the bridge of his nose. This definitely wasn't good.

"I understand if you've changed your mind," said Eramus. "You don't have to explain. I'll just—"

Eramus turned to walk away, but Ordin gripped his shoulder, his expression pained. "I haven't changed my mind, or at least I didn't want to. Arnan came to visit me earlier. He threatened to..." Ordin's eyes glazed, and it took several moments for him to continue. "He threatened to burn down the mill if I allowed you to stay."

"What!"

Heat flooded over Eramus's body. How could Arnan, the man meant to prioritize the village's best interests, threaten to destroy not only Ordin's livelihood, but the thing that helped all the people who lived here? Sure, they could grind the wheat by hand, but the process would require more time and more people. There simply weren't enough free bodies to accomplish the task and keep up with everything else the village needed.

"How could he do such a thing?" Eramus muttered. "He'd be punishing everyone."

Ordin shook his head. "I know, and I hope you will forgive me. Arnan may be the leader, but I don't dare assume his threat was empty. He seems to resent you, and I cannot risk losing the mill. It's too important to our community."

"No, it's not a risk worth taking. I'm sorry he threatened you at all. I'm sorry I can't help you."

"Perhaps one day he'll come to his senses," said Ordin. "I'd have you back in an instant."

"I appreciate that more than you know. I'd best leave in case Arnan's watching."

Eramus left Ordin standing in the mill with a frown. He needed to get out of there before his emotions got the better of him. A mixture of anger and sadness spread over his body, causing his skin to prickle. He focused on his steps. Allowing his emotions to control him would only draw out his power with unbridled force. Arnan was waiting for him to make a mistake and unleashing a wave of untamed magic inside the village would qualify.

He marched towards the grassy plain where flowers still dotted the landscape. He could release his magic freely here, without concern of mishaps. Eramus stopped in the center of the meadow and drew a deep breath. He closed his eyes. Warmth spread through his arms, but before he could do anything with the blue light that surrounded his hands, a soft voice filled his ears.

"I thought you were working at the mill today?"

His heart lurched. Evree stood just a few yards away, her hands clasped behind her back. She smiled, and the negative emotions immediately drained from him. "Evree. I..." Should he tell her? Arnan was her uncle, after all. The last thing he wanted was to create more drama. Besides, him getting upset about the situation was exactly what the man wanted.

"Turns out Ordin isn't ready to process the wheat just yet."

He hated lying to her, but he knew Evree. She wouldn't let her uncle's slight go unpunished. She'd have the entire village in an uproar. He loved how spirited she was, but now wasn't the time for it, not when the display would cause more problems than it solved.

"How fortunate for me," she said, closing the space between them.

Eramus mussed his hair. He was happy to see her, but had hoped she would forgo coming to the meadow today. Morzaun could appear at any moment, and he didn't trust the man enough to feel comfortable having Evree nearby.

"Evree, I've loved spending time with you the last few days, but...perhaps it would be best if you weren't here when I practiced my magic. The last thing I want is for you to get hurt. My powers are a little chaotic at times."

"Only when you're upset." Her eyes narrowed. "Are you upset?"

Blast.

Having mentioned the effect his emotions had on his abilities a few days ago, he now realized his foolish mistake.

She folded her arms and raised her brows at his hesitation. "All right. Spit it out, Eramus. *Something* has you upset. I demand to know what it is."

Eramus chewed his cheek. If she wasn't so adorable when chiding him, perhaps he could have resisted her command, but one look from her could convince him to do anything. "Ordin ended my apprenticeship. Your uncle threatened to burn the mill if he didn't comply."

Evree's eye twitched. Eramus placed his hands on her shoulders. "Listen, I need you to go home. Just for today, I need some time to practice without you here. Please."

Evree growled. "When I tell my father about this—"

"No! You mustn't tell anyone!"

"Rotten apples, I'm not! He can't do this. I won't stand by..." She spun around, her hands clenched as she marched with determination towards the village.

Eramus darted in front of her and placed his hands on her upper arms, blocking her progress. "Evree, you can't go back!"

She scowled. "I thought you wanted me to go back?"

He groaned. "Yes, but not like this!"

"This isn't fair. He can't treat you this way!"

Eramus moved his hands to her cheeks without thinking. Her green eyes went wide, and she gasped. "We will figure this out," he whispered. "I promise. But not today. I will endure Arnan's attempts to intimidate me, but I refuse to put us in jeopardy."

"Us?" she mumbled.

He nodded. His gaze fell to her lips, and his pulse quickened. Her lavender scent drew him in, inching his face closer to hers. Evree leaned forward.

"My timing is clearly not the best."

Morzaun's deep voice froze Eramus before their lips could touch. Poor timing, indeed.

Evree pulled away, her narrowed eyes looking Morzaun over with suspicion. "Who are you?"

Morzaun smirked. "A friend."

Evree tucked herself behind Eramus, her trembling fingers clasping his arm. Eramus placed his hand over hers. "He's here to help with my magic, to teach me better control."

She looked up at him with concern. "You know him?"

Eramus rubbed the back of his neck. "Well...sort of."

Her brows drew together, and her nose scrunched. "What is that supposed to mean?"

"Perhaps I should introduce myself to your friend," said Morzaun. He stepped closer and stretched his hand towards her. Evree flinched. Eramus couldn't blame her for being apprehensive, and the man's dark attire did nothing to help. Black fabric covered nearly every inch of his body, and he wore a chest plate as though he waited for battle.

"My name is Morzaun," he said, his hand hovering at Eramus's side.

Evree hesitated for a moment before accepting it. Her voice was so soft, it was almost inaudible. "Evree."

Morzaun bowed and then backed away. "A pleasure." He turned his focus to Eramus, and his lips pulled upwards on one side. "Shall we get started?"

Eramus glanced down at Evree. Her gaze remained fixed on the man who was still practically a stranger. He didn't want her to stay, not when he didn't fully trust Morzaun or his own power. "Evree, please go back to the village. I will see you tomorrow."

He earned his second scowl for the day. "Absolutely not. I'm staying."

Shooting her a pointed look did nothing. She released her grip on his arm and planted her hands firmly on her hips. Morzaun chuckled.

"All right," said Eramus after an exasperated sigh. "But sit by the tree line. I don't want you anywhere near me while I'm practicing."

Evree gathered her skirts and marched across the meadow with her chin held high. Eramus shook his head. That girl might be the death of him.

"She's rather tenacious," said Morzaun, lifting one of his brows.

Eramus cleared his throat. The last thing he wanted to discuss was his relationship with Evree. "What do you intend to teach me first?"

"There are many spells I can teach you, but we'll start with some simple ones. The first is called the *illustris*."

Eramus's face crumpled. "The spells have names?"

Morzaun laughed. "Yes, they do. When the three children first trained with their magic, they practiced their skills as you have—without knowledge of incantations. But over time, something guided them to understand the language of the Virgàm, making spells much easier to learn...and teach."

"Something guided them?"

He nodded. "When the children first arrived at the base of Kantinar, it is said that a strange voice led them up the mountain, directing them to the Virgàm. After the scepter bestowed them magic, it continued to guide the children by instructing them to compile a book of spells. The voice presented the language to one of them through visions, and it was then taught to the other magic wielders."

"And this voice, where does it come from...or who does it belong to?"

Morzaun tilted his head, a bemused grin stretching across his face. "That is an excellent question, and one I have no answer for." He held his hands in front of him, palms facing the sky. "Now, the *illustris.*"

Eramus copied Morzaun's instruction, repeating odd words that knotted his tongue. It took several attempts, but eventually a blue orb settled above his palm, glowing as bright as the sun.

"Well done," said Morzaun. "The *illustris* is a useful spell. One never knows when they might find themselves amidst the darkness."

Eramus lifted the orb into the air, watching it glisten in the sunlight. He clenched his hand, and the blue orb flattened and dispersed until no trace of it remained. "What's next?"

For several hours, Morzaun taught him simple spells, some of which Eramus had unwittingly used before. Now, they had a name, and knowing the incantations allowed him to conjure them with more power and ease. By late afternoon, exhaustion claimed him.

"I didn't realize how much energy magic required," he said between gasps.

Morzaun gripped his shoulder. "You'll get used to it with practice. Now that you no longer hide your abilities, your power will grow." He reached inside his cloak and pulled the round amulet from inside.

"You're leaving?" asked Eramus. Part of him saddened. He still had so many questions, but as his thoughts turned to Evree, he realized now wasn't the best time for them. He preferred his self-discovery was done in private. Who knew what secrets lay buried in his past.

"I'll see you again in a few days. Until then, keep practicing."

The gem in the center of the amulet illuminated. Morzaun's body slowly disappeared, turning to dust before his eyes.

Evree bounded towards him, holding her skirts with one hand and her bonnet in place with the other. "He just disappeared!"

Eramus shrugged when she stopped in front of him. "He has a tendency to do that."

She bit her lip and writhed her fingers together. "Eramus, are you certain you can trust that man? Something about him...I just don't know."

He sighed. She was right, and his instincts hoisted red flags. But

Morzaun had information Eramus needed, and he couldn't allow the opportunity to slip through his fingers.

"I don't have any choice but to trust him right now. If he can teach me to control my power, it may help our people feel more comfortable. And, he claims to have knowledge about my family. I need answers, Evree. I need to know who I am."

Evree moved to his side and wrapped her hand around his arm. "Just promise you'll be careful. I can't stand the thought of you getting hurt."

"I'll be careful, but I would prefer you weren't here when Morzaun is around. At least not until we know for certain we can trust him. I want you to stay in the village where it's safe. Will you do that for me?"

Her nose wrinkled. "I suppose I will, but I don't like the idea of you being out here alone with him. What if he's some sort of ruffian?"

Eramus chuckled. "I think I can handle myself if he is. He doesn't have magic and I do."

"He may still be dangerous. I could be your guard? Step in if things get out of hand."

She stared up at him with the most serious expression, but Eramus couldn't help but smile. The notion that she could take on a man of Morzaun's form was ridiculous, but he had to give her bravery due credit.

"What would you actually do?" he asked, tucking a lock of hair behind her ear.

Evree thought for a moment. "Punch him in the nose?"

He tilted his head back and laughed. "I've no doubt you would, but ease my trepidation and keep your punches to yourself for now? Stay home, Evree. Please."

She rolled her eyes and nodded. "Very well."

"May I walk you back?"

She fought a smile, but it slipped through anyway. "You may."

As they neared the village, Evree pulled him to a stop and slid her hand from his arm. "Will Morzaun return tomorrow?"

Eramus shook his head. "In a few days."

She averted her gaze and stepped closer to him. "Am I allowed to come to the meadow, then? We were interrupted this morning."

They certainly were. Morzaun's appearance had disrupted a moment Eramus had imagined for a long time. Although time had claimed that kiss, he was hopeful he'd have another chance, and Evree seemed to feel the same way.

"Tomorrow in the meadow," he said with a smile. "Perhaps we can pick up where we left off."

She grinned, and without a word, walked back to the village. Eramus watched until she disappeared between two cottages, unable to stop himself from smiling.

As he started forward, a figure caught his eye. Arnan glared at him from where he leaned against the wooden fence of the horse corral with folded arms, his fierce gaze burning like a wild blaze.

CHAPTER NINE
Reclaimed Memories

The images flew past him like flashes of lighting. The gardens with the stone birds stretched before him and the same men offered a parade of taunts until a wave of blue light sent them hurtling to the ground.

Eramus moved, following the course of his memories as though he were reliving them. He turned the corner of the marble wall, crashing into the man with stern eyes. His hands gripped Eramus's shoulders, preventing him from escaping.

His uncle, or so the man claimed, towered over him with a wide smirk. A velvet cape draped over his shoulders and attached to his black tunic with golden plates. His honey brown hair parted neatly to one side, and he smelled of leather and pine.

"Come now, Eramus. You can tell your uncle. It will be our little secret."

"Let me go!"

The man's grip tightened, sending pain down his arms. "You *will* tell me, or I will lock you and your mother in the dungeon. I only desire an answer, Eramus. Do not make me punish her for your disobedience."

Eramus's eyes glazed, and his voice came out as a whisper. "Only a few months."

He shoved Eramus against the wall, and the stone scraped against his head. "That wasn't so difficult, now was it? This power of yours...it's unnatural, a curse upon humanity. But we will put it to good use. Izarden will be stronger than ever before."

"I don't want to help you!"

The man leaned in close, his face inches from Eramus. "I'm not giving you a choice. If you prefer your mother alive, then I suggest you cooperate. Your father may have betrayed his kingdom, but I'm offering you the opportunity to rectify his misdeeds. You should thank me."

"He wasn't the traitor. You are!"

A hard slap left his face stinging. "Those are the words of your mother," the man said, jabbing a finger into Eramus's chest. "If she knows what's best for her, she'll quit filling your head with such nonsense." He grabbed Eramus's chin and forced him to meet his gaze. "Run along now, Eramus. And when I call for you, I expect your compliance. Do I make myself clear?"

Eramus bolted. He entered the large marble structure and

darted down corridors, his sense of familiarity growing. Banners of deep purple lined the walls, all bearing the image of a black bird, and the letters Z and I embroidered in their centers.

He clambered up a small flight of stairs and ran to the end of a long hallway. Eramus slammed the door closed behind him before crumbling to the ground and pulling his knees to his chest. His tears flowed without restraint, and his body trembled.

Flowers. The sweet scent filled his nostrils, and his heart calmed with the recognition of her smell. Warm hands pulled him in close, and he leaned against his mother as her arms encompassed him. Rubbing his back, she cooed, her voice easing his sobs.

"What is it, my love? Tell me what's wrong."

"He knows," Eramus answered between sniffles. "Uncle Sytal knows."

For several moments, she stayed quiet. When she finally spoke, her arms tightened around him, and her voice cracked. "Are you certain?"

Eramus nodded. "He says I have to do what he tells me or he'll punish you...lock us in the dungeon." He pulled away from her and stared up into her warm amber eyes. "I hate him. He's a monster and...and I don't want to hurt other people. What if he makes me?"

His mother tilted her head, tears rolling over her cheeks. She wiped his with the back of her hand. "I won't let that happen. I promise. Your uncle will not control you. I'm going to make sure of it."

Eramus shook his head. "He'll hurt you—"

"Don't you worry about me," she said, patting his cheek with her hand. "Your father and I knew this day would come. We have a plan." She sighed and turned towards the window on the opposite side of the room. "I just hoped for more time. Zeeran was nearly ten before...it doesn't matter. All you need to know is that everything is going to be all right."

A soft knock made him flinch. "Come in," said his mother, her tone calm and even.

A young woman with golden brown hair peeked around the door. Her forehead furrowed when her gaze found them sitting on the floor. "Forgive me for intruding, Princess. Did you want to take tea this afternoon?"

His mother shook her head. "No, Irena, but your timing is perfect. I need your help."

Irena entered the room and closed the door, drawing her brows tighter together. "Your Highness?"

Eramus glanced at his mother. The sadness in her eyes made his heart ache. "I need you to take Eramus away from Izarden," she whispered. "I need you to keep him safe."

* * *

Eramus stared out his window, watching the sun peek over the mountains. His thoughts wandered over the memories the night had presented. He'd seen his mother. For the first time in over a decade he knew her face, recognized the sound of her voice. She had wanted to protect him from his uncle and planned to send him away.

His uncle. *Sytal.* The information made his heart race. At first, Eramus thought the name was nothing more than coincidence, but the young handmaiden had confirmed the truth, addressing his mother as *princess* and *your highness.* Royalty flowed through his blood, and Eramus had once lived at the palace in Izarden.

He ran his fingers through his hair. Trying to piece together his past was frustrating. His mother had sent him away to keep him from his uncle's grasp, and based on his previous dreams, Eramus concluded his journey with the young handmaiden had ended in disaster. The ship had capsized into the sea, and he could only speculate that his family presumed him dead.

But why had his mother not gone with him? Why had she chosen to stay? And his father...where was he?

Eramus groaned. He might never have all the answers, but he knew where to start. He needed to see Morzaun.

Three days had passed since Morzaun trained Eramus in the meadow. He had hoped to spend time with Evree until the man returned, but Arnan had stolen her attention...or at least tried to. Her uncle put every excuse he knew into play, asking for help with the apple harvest and begging her to accompany the field workers. But his efforts didn't stop Evree from passing Eramus coy smiles or occasional winks. Arnan had even caught her a time or two, and the deep scowls that followed made them both laugh.

With Evree preoccupied, Eramus spent his time searching for work with no success. Too many of the villagers distrusted him, and Eramus suspected Arnan may have put out a warning against his hire.

But today, Eramus would go to the meadow and speak with Morzaun. He still preferred that Evree wasn't around when the man appeared, so Arnan's intervention would prove beneficial for now.

"You're off again, are you?" asked Inara, her brows raised. He'd yet to tell her about Morzaun, mostly because he didn't want her to worry. Meeting with a stranger alone in the meadow wasn't exactly the wisest decision he'd ever made.

"Afraid so. Since I can't work, I figured practicing my magic wouldn't hurt. I just want to have better control over it."

She nodded, but her lips pursed. "Don't understand why Arnan is so insistent on making your life miserable. You've done nothing to deserve it."

Eramus chuckled and kissed her cheek. "Everything will be fine, Mother. Don't worry yourself over it."

He bid her goodbye and made his way to the meadow. The sun warmed his skin and the stuffy air stole his breath. Morzaun was waiting when he arrived, standing in the shaded grass beneath the oaks in his usual black attire.

"Ah, Eramus. I hope you are well?"

He wasn't sure how to answer that. Between his frustrations with the villagers and the unanswered questions, his mood could be better. "I'm fine."

Morzaun's brows flew to the top of his forehead. "Something is bothering you?"

Eramus chewed his cheek for a moment. "My people don't trust me. I've lost the only work I had...my future livelihood. Evree's uncle intends to send me away, and I'm bombarded every night with dreams I don't understand." The words spilled so quickly from his lips he was gasping by the time he finished.

Morzaun sighed. "Well, I can't offer advice on how your village treats you. People have never been accepting of our power, but perhaps I can provide some guidance about these dreams. What is it you see in them?"

"I used my power against several men. They were taunting me about my father, calling him a traitor. Another man stopped me when I ran away, said he was my uncle. He wanted to use my power for his own purposes. My mother..." He choked on the word. Eramus couldn't remember anything about her beyond what he saw in his dreams, but in those brief moments, he had felt her love. "She sent me away to protect me from him."

"You saw your mother?" Morzaun's eyes darkened. "Did you learn anything else in this dream?"

"A woman addressed my mother as *princess*. She was royalty. *I'm* royalty."

Eramus glanced at Morzaun. His expression displayed no astonishment. How could the revelation not come as a surprise? Unless he already knew. Morzaun was more aware of his past than he had let on.

"I want you to tell me what you know," said Eramus.

Morzaun met his gaze. "You're better off not knowing."

Warmth flooded through his body, and his hands balled into fists. "I'm sick of not knowing who I am! Why do you hesitate? Why keep the information from me? I have a right to know what happened to my family."

Morzaun placed his hand on the trunk of the thick oak and pressed his fingers into the deep grooves of the bark. "I don't wish to cause you more pain, Eramus, but if you insist on having the details, then I will give them to you."

Eramus relaxed. All he wanted was to understand himself, and the answers seemed just out of his reach. "I'm sorry. I don't mean to demand it from you, but I've never been so close to having answers. Any information you share brings me that much closer to the truth."

Morzaun considered him for a moment and then nodded. "Before you were born, your uncle inherited the throne of Izarden. Sytal was nothing like his father. He desired power, and he sacrificed countless lives to get it. He demanded your father use his power to expand our kingdom, to overthrow the other kings of Virgamor and unite our land under his supreme rule. Your father refused. Sytal banished him, but because he feared the power your father possessed, he held your mother captive as insurance."

"So, my father's abandonment was an effort to protect her?"

"Yes, and to protect you. For eight years the two of you lived at the palace in Izarden under tight watch. Unbeknownst to Sytal, your mother sent correspondences to your father regularly. She kept him informed of Sytal's plans and acts of war, and your father even took to disrupting a few of them."

Eramus moved to stand beside him and placed his hand on the rough bark of the tree. "That's why they called him a traitor."

"I suppose that is part of it," said Morzaun. "When Sytal found out you could wield magic like your father, he intended to force you to do his bidding. Your mother, Senniva, refused to allow that to happen, so she sent you away with one of her handmaidens."

"In my dreams, I see a ship lost to the sea, and Inara said she found me washed up on shore. I kept wondering why my mother didn't go with me, but if she had, she would have drowned with everyone else. It is better that she didn't."

"I wish that were true, Eramus." He sat down on a fallen log a few feet away, his expression heavy with sadness. "Senniva sent your father a note, explaining her plan to send you away from Izarden, away from your uncle. She believed you had a better chance if she didn't go with you. Senniva was the princess. The people knew her and would have recognized her wherever she went, so she remained behind.

"When Sytal discovered what she had done, he demanded to know where you were. Your mother refused to tell him, and her life ended by his hand."

"Sytal killed my mother because she protected me?"

"I told you I did not wish to cause you more pain."

Eramus nodded and attempted to swallow the lump that had settled in his throat. "And my father?"

"Alive. Sytal's son continues to search for him. After Senniva's death, your father sought justice. I assume even you have heard the rumors of King Sytal's demise?"

Eramus froze. "You mean the army and the death of the king...my father did that?"

"Yes."

His heart pounded. The stories of a dark sorcerer decimating the army of Izarden were not only true, but the work of his own father. Eramus had never imagined his past would be so complicated. Murder, bloodshed, and a fight for power—it all overwhelmed him. He collapsed to the ground, his body trembling.

Morzaun crouched beside him and placed a firm hand on his shoulder. "Listen to me, Eramus. Your village knows about your power. If word reaches King Delran that you are here, he will not hesitate to send his army to find you. That is why I have come—to prepare you."

"I've done nothing to the king," said Eramus. "All I want is to live here in peace."

"I don't think it's possible, at least not in perpetuity. Word will reach him, Eramus. You need to be ready when it does."

Eramus nodded. If the new king was anything like Sytal, he would stop at nothing to eradicate the magic that killed his father, and Delran might put the entire village in jeopardy to get to him. Inara, Evree...all the people he cared about would be at risk. He had to master his power. It was the only way to protect those he loved.

"So, what are we waiting for?" said Eramus. "Teach me everything you know."

CHAPTER TEN
Estranged Family

Eramus lifted a large sack from the wagon onto his shoulder. He hauled it through the door and tossed it on top of the pile of burlap bags in the corner, sending a cloud of fine dust into the air. Returning to the wagon, he wiped the sweat from his brow before lifting another. Having carried twenty sacks into the bakery already, his muscles protested the exertion.

For the last two days, Eramus had assisted the village baker, Thermak, when flour arrived from the mill. He had Ordin to thank for the temporary work. Without the man's recommendation, Eramus might have never found a job, and although Thermak agreed to the arrangement, he had clarified that Eramus would keep things hushed.

With the flour unloaded, Eramus wandered into the bakery in search of Thermak. It didn't take long to find him, as he stood a few feet inside the door, his brown eyes watching Eramus's every move.

"All finished," said Eramus with as much cheer in his voice as he could manage.

Thermak grunted and removed a few coins from the cloth pouch hanging at his waist. "Here," he said, thrusting them into Eramus's hand. "Shop will be open soon."

Eramus nodded. That was Thermak's way of saying he needed to leave. With Arnan's warning, no one in the village wanted to hire him. Thermak was taking a risk, and Eramus couldn't blame the man for urging him to leave before people took notice.

Walking through the village grew easier with each passing day. Fewer people darted away upon seeing him, and some even offered him small, polite smiles. It wasn't the same as before—it would never be—but any progress was better than nothing.

He turned the corner and froze. Two covered wagons blocked his path, and Arnan stood at the rear of them. Soon, he and a small group would leave to sell the apple harvest at the coast. Eramus welcomed a few days without the man constantly glaring at him. Perhaps he would even get a few moments alone with Evree.

Eramus turned to retreat, but it was too late; Arnan had already spotted him.

"Just a second, Eramus! You and I need to have a word."

Eramus's fists automatically clenched. He drew a deep breath and spun around. "What do we need to talk about?"

Arnan was close...too close. "You know very well what. I'm

leaving for Olgetha, and you better stay away from my niece. Don't think I'm not watching you even while I'm gone. I always have eyes on my village."

"I'm happy to stay away from Evree when she asks me to," said Eramus, his fingers digging into his palms. "It's not your place to dictate what she can and cannot do."

"Perhaps I need to have a discussion with my brother before I go?"

Eramus scoffed and shook his head. "Because that went so well last time?"

A fist connected with his face, striking between his nose and upper lip and sending his body to the ground. Warm liquid flowed from his nose, and the back of his head throbbed. Arnan towered over him with a wide smirk, his tall figure engulfing him in shadow. "I'll see you soon, Eramus."

Eramus pushed himself from the ground just in time to watch Arnan climb into the wagon. Both carts pulled forward and disappeared out of sight. He wiped his nose with the back of his hand, coating it in crimson. Arnan had attempted to push him to the breaking point, but Eramus would not allow the man the satisfaction. He refused to give his people any reason to consider his banishment.

He wiped his nose several times before arriving home, staining his skin even more red. Arnan had socked him good. He pushed open the cottage door, and in seconds, Inara was at his side, fussing over his bloody state.

"What in Virgamor happened! I thought you were working for

Thermak this morning?"

Eramus massaged the bridge of his nose and closed his eyes. His vision was a bit fuzzy, and his head throbbed. He could do with a nap. "I was, but Arnan demanded a discussion with me before he left for Olgetha."

Her forehead furrowed. "I'm sure that didn't go well." Eramus pointed to his nose, and she sighed. "He can't continue treating you this way. It isn't right."

"As the village leader, he can treat me however he wishes."

She wrinkled her nose. "Well, no one nominated him. The man just assumed the position, and I'm willing to bet few people actually want him at that particular post." She crossed her arms, grumbling. "Perhaps a leech collector or manure sweeper would be more suitable."

Eramus chuckled. "Can't say I disagree."

Inara glanced up at him with glazed eyes and took his hand. "Come, let's get you cleaned up. We have company, after all."

"Company?"

His eyes darted around the room and landed on two blurry figures before she could answer. He squinted, forcing his eyes to focus. They sat at the wooden table, a man and a woman, both wearing smiles that stretched the width of their faces. The woman stood and flicked her long, blonde hair over her shoulder before clasping her hands at her waist.

"Hello, Eramus," she said, her voice melodically cheerful.

His pulse quickened. Who were these people, and why had Inara allowed them into their home? Morzaun had warned him that the king would send his army upon the village once he learned Eramus resided here. Despite having finally revealed his power, he needed to keep it a secret from the rest of Virgamor...for everyone's sake. Having strangers in his home only complicated the situation. The more people that knew about his power, the more likely the information would reach King Delran.

"Who are you?"

The man rose and joined the woman at her side. He wrapped his arm around her shoulders, and she gave him a small nod. "My name is Aldeth," he said. "I'm your uncle, and this is my wife, Yelene."

Eramus retreated to the door. The only uncle he was aware of had killed his mother, and though this man could not possibly be the deceased king, Eramus refused to trust him.

Aldeth held his palms out. "It's all right, Eramus. We aren't here to hurt you."

Yelene stepped forward, her eyes pleading. "Please don't be afraid. We've searched for you for a long time. I saw the ship lost to the sea and feared the worst, but we never gave up hope of finding you."

"Saw?"

His stomach rolled. What did she mean by that?

Aldeth gestured towards the table. "Please, sit. We will explain everything to you. I give you my word."

Inara patted his arm. "I feel we can trust them, dear. You've waited so long for answers. It's time you found some."

Little did she know he had already received many. So many

times he'd considered telling Inara about Morzaun, but something stopped him. If the king of Izarden was searching for him, the less Inara knew, the better. Eramus glanced at Yelene, whose hopeful eyes beamed back at him with such warmth that the tension in his body eased. He didn't trust them, but Eramus also couldn't deny his curiosity. He moved to the table and pulled out a chair.

Aldeth and Yelene sat down across from him, while Inara busied herself near the washbasin. She returned a few seconds later with a small, wet rag and offered it to him. Eramus passed her a perplexed expression and her brows raised. "Your nose."

His hand moved subconsciously to where Arnan's fist had landed. Eramus had nearly forgotten about the incident, what with two strangers in his home claiming to be family.

He took the cloth and wiped his face, leaving it with streaks of dark red. "Thank you, Mother."

She patted his shoulder and sat down beside him. When no one spoke, Eramus took to querying for information. "What did you mean by you *saw* the ship fall into the sea? No one survived but me...or at least I didn't think they did."

"Yelene is a Seer," said Aldeth. "She saw the ship in a vision, and later, that you washed ashore. We searched for you for weeks, but it seems someone else found you first." He turned to Inara and smiled. "We couldn't be more grateful that you've cared for him all this time."

Eramus scratched the back of his head. "What do you mean, she's a Seer? Has visions? Can you wield magic?"

Aldeth nodded. "Yes, we can both use magic. Although, ours

differs from your own. Inara told us your aura is blue. Is that right?"

Eramus chewed his cheek. What difference did that make? Was magic not always blue? Morzaun's gemstones had all presented a blue glow.

"Yes. That's correct."

Aldeth smiled. "I know you must have questions, so I will do my best to answer." He held up his hand, and after a moment, green light danced around it. Eramus's eyes went wide. "A green aura," continued Aldeth, "signifies that one is an Elementalist, whereas blue, like your own, identifies one as a Protesta. There are three magical abilities, Eramus, each one with its own strengths. An Elementalist has control over the earth, water, wind...even animals. A Protesta can produce the strongest spells and learning them is much easier."

"The Seer is the third." He nodded to Yelene. A purple glow surrounded her hand as it hovered over the table. "Yelene's ability allows her to see the future."

"That's how we found you," said Yelene. "I had a vision. It took some time to identify exactly where you were, but we came as soon as we knew."

Eramus massaged his forehead, the information overwhelming him. Magic was far more complicated than he had ever imagined, but what pressed on him more were the details Morzaun had shared about the Virgàm. He said Eramus's father was one of the original users of magic, that three children had found the scepter hidden away on Mt. Kantinar. Eramus suspected he knew who the other two children were.

"Tell me about the Virgàm," said Eramus.

Yelene and Aldeth exchanged looks of surprise.

"The what?" asked Inara.

"It's a scepter," Eramus answered. "The source of magic in humans."

Yelene tilted her head, her brows drawn tight. "How did you know that?"

Perhaps he shouldn't have said anything. He still didn't know if he could trust them. He didn't know if he could trust Morzaun. But something in his gut made him regret revealing his knowledge.

Eramus leaned forward. "I want to know why you're here. Why did you come looking for me?"

Aldeth's eyes narrowed, but he didn't voice any suspicion with the change of subject. "You're family, Eramus. We only want to keep you safe. Your father...he's put a target on your back because of the things he's done. King Delran seeks revenge, and if he discovers your whereabouts, he will stop at nothing to kill you."

Inara's sharp gasp made Eramus's stomach lurch. He didn't want her to worry, but with this second confirmation, Eramus knew they spoke the truth. His presence in the village put everyone in danger of the king's wrath.

"We came to get you," said Yelene. She leaned across the table and placed her hand over his. "We came to take you home."

Eramus looked up into her bright blue eyes. Warmth flooded over him. Desperation constricted his chest. He wanted to believe them.

"You'll be safe with us," she whispered. "King Delran can't get to you on Verascene."

Verascene. Treacherous waters surrounded the island off the coast of Izarden. Even the bravest captains dared not go near the jagged rocks and shallows. No one had access to the place, and once stranded, no one ever left. Then again, if Aldeth had control over the elements, rough seas proved no issue. Perhaps he and Yelene could come and go as they pleased.

He would be safe in such a place, but his heart ached at the idea of leaving. What about Inara? What about Evree? He wasn't sure he could leave everything he'd ever known behind.

Yelene's hand tightened around his own, pulling him from his thoughts. "Please come with us," she said, her pleading tone returning.

"I..." His heart raced. How was he to make this decision? He turned to Inara and found her eyes full of tears.

"You should consider it, dear. If what they say is true...if you are truly in danger..." Her voice trailed off into a sob. Eramus pulled his hand away from Yelene and wrapped his arm around his mother. She leaned into his shoulder. "All I ever wanted was to keep you safe, even if it means I never see you again."

Her tears pierced his heart, pulling out his own. "I don't know if I can. I don't want to leave you."

"I know this is difficult," said Aldeth. "But I ask that you take some time to consider it. Delran is not a man to be trifled with."

Eramus sighed and nodded. "I will." All eyes followed him as he rose. "I need some time alone. Please excuse me."

The door to the cottage closed with a soft thud. With so much to process, there was only one place he wanted to go. In the meadow's solitude, he could think clearly. He could make the most difficult decision of his life.

CHAPTER ELEVEN
Sparring with Magic

Twirling the stem between his fingers, Eramus held up the tiny flower, its color as bright as the sun. Buttercups, Evree had called them. He couldn't help but think of her as he studied the soft golden petals. Would there be buttercups on Verascene?

His stomach twisted so violently he thought he might spill whatever remained of his breakfast over the dark green grass. The thought of leaving filled him with unprecedented dread. How could he leave the people who had become strangers to live with the strangers that claimed to be family? He wasn't sure he could.

But leaving made the most sense. If Eramus removed himself from the village, his people would be safe. Verascene would keep him out of King Delran's reach, but it would also take him away from everything he cared about.

"It isn't fair," he muttered. "I've done nothing to deserve him hunting me like some animal."

"Life is rarely fair."

Eramus turned. Near the tree line, a man leaned against a tall oak with folded arms and a smug grin. Unlike Eramus's regular company, he wore a simple dark green tunic and brown trousers, and his disheveled black hair moved with the gentle breeze.

The man, who appeared not much older than Eramus, pushed away from the trunk and took a few steps towards him. "Born with the abilities the likes of which the world has never seen, the power to save Virgamor from the destruction of selfish men, and yet we are the ones hunted. Hated. They will never appreciate us for what we are. Respect and acceptance...they are meaningless to people like us."

He stopped a few feet away and stared out over the meadow. Eramus clenched his jaw. He was growing tired of strangers constantly showing up in his life and had certainly had his fill for one day. "Who are you?"

The man chuckled. "He said you would be suspicious. I suppose I can't blame you for that, not with the way your people have treated you."

"He? You mean Morzaun?"

"Yes. He'll be joining us soon, but I think he sensed you needed guidance. Unfortunately, he thought I would make a suitable substitute until he could come himself." He laughed and shook his head. "But I'm no good at this sort of thing."

Knowing Morzaun sent the man provided Eramus with little comfort. "And why would he send you in the first place?"

"We are family," answered the man. "That must count for something." His outstretched hand made Eramus's stomach knot. "The name's Zeeran."

That name. His mother had mentioned it in his dream. What had she said? *Zeeran was nearly ten...* At the time, Eramus hadn't known what she meant, too focused on understanding the lost memories invading his mind, but now he wondered if she was referring to magic. Eramus had gained the ability to wield magic when he was eight; it seemed Zeeran had been slightly older.

"You can use magic," said Eramus, ignoring Zeeran's attempt at pleasantries. "My mother spoke of you."

"Did she? Nice things, I hope? I always liked Aunt Senniva. Shame I didn't come to know her better before...well, you understand. Boils my blood, what happened. But Sytal got what he deserved in the end."

Eramus's head reeled. He massaged his temple, hoping to ease the throbbing, remnants of his tussle with Arnan. "My mother was your aunt?"

Zeeran snorted. "That is how the whole cousin deal works."

"You're my cousin?"

Zeeran spoke plainly, but Eramus struggled to comprehend his words. His head injury probably had something to do with it, but the unprecedented amount of information he'd received in the last hour didn't help either.

An exasperated sigh drew his attention. "Yes, Eramus. I was under the impression Morzaun had cleared this part up, but it appears I am mistaken. Your father and my mother were siblings. You were told about the three children who found the Virgàm, were you not?"

Eramus nodded. Of those details, he was aware. He even thought he knew their identities.

"Right. So, there was your father and both of my parents. They are the original wielders of magic. Passed their abilities on to us, although we are not nearly as strong as they are. Bit frustrating, that."

"Yelene and Aldeth are your parents?"

The color drained from Zeeran's face, and Eramus immediately regretted the words. Morzaun had told him nothing of his aunt and uncle, and he couldn't shake the feeling that there was a reason for the negligence.

Zeeran's eyes narrowed, and suspicion filled his tone. "That's correct. But how did you—"

A soft whizzing cut him off. In a moment, Morzaun's body materialized before them. He clenched the round amulet in his hand, the blue glow fading once the black dust had all swirled into place.

"Ah, Eramus. I was hoping Zeeran would find you."

"Showed up a few minutes after I did," said Zeeran, his head tilted and his perplexed expression still studying Eramus.

Morzaun smiled. "Very good. I've wished for the two of you to meet for a while."

"Then why didn't you mention him, or my aunt and uncle?

Why does it feel as though you are hiding things from me?"

The sigh that escaped Morzaun was heavy and accompanied by sympathetic eyes. "I never wanted to overwhelm you. Between training and the details of your past, I feared it would be too much to tell you everything at once. Forgive me. I only have your best interests at heart."

Eramus wanted to believe him. Morzaun had given him the truth when he needed it most. But he also couldn't ignore his instincts. *Something* left him uneasy.

"I thought Zeeran could assist with your training today," said Morzaun. "Unlike me, he can wield magic. Some spells are much easier to learn when you have a proper example."

Zeeran moved to stand opposite them, tapping his finger to his chin. "Where should we start, then? I know." He held up his palms, and a blue aura surrounded them. "The *impetras* will do."

"Zeeran." The warning in Morzaun's tone suggested this wasn't a spell Eramus wanted to learn, at least not from his cousin.

"Just a bit of fun. I'll go easy on him."

Before Eramus could rebuff, a wave of blue light flowed towards him and crashed into his chest. His body flew backwards a dozen yards, and he landed on the grass, his head smacking against the ground. He gasped. The attack had knocked the wind out of him, not to mention the throbbing on the back of his head grew worse.

"Zeeran!" Morzaun's black cape glided behind him as the gap between him and the man vanished. Morzaun gripped him by the collar and yanked him closer, a deathly glare in his eyes. "This isn't a game. He isn't ready for that."

His cousin smirked. "The best way to get him ready is to knock him on his rear a few times. It was always great motivation for me."

"You've trained since you were ten. Had your father and I to guide you, not to mention Ladisias." Morzaun shoved him and jabbed a finger into his chest. "Don't do it again."

Eramus propped himself up on his elbows. Watching the two's interactions made his heart race. Zeeran seemed to hold some sort of grudge against Eramus, although why, he didn't know. They'd only met a few minutes ago.

"I don't recall you being so overprotective when you trained Ladisias," said Zeeran as Morzaun walked away. "You certainly didn't show me such mercy, not that you trained me much before you disappeared. No surprise you would go easy on *him*."

He nodded in Eramus's direction. Morzaun spat. "Watch your words, Zeeran. If you don't like the way I do things, then go home. Go back to Verascene."

Zeeran had left Verascene? Why? Perhaps he shouldn't concern himself with it at all, but their squabble did nothing to ease his concerns.

Muttering, Zeeran turned away from them. Morzaun offered Eramus a hand and pulled him from the ground. "A shield spell. You've used one before, and"—Eramus opened his mouth to interrupt, but Morzaun stopped him—"I was watching you, remember? I know you can conjure a decent shield. An attack like that would be a good time to make use of the knowledge."

Eramus clenched his jaw and nodded. How much time had

Morzaun spent watching him? The thought sent chills through his body.

"Conjure your shield, and then Zeeran can send a *small* amount of energy towards you." Morzaun glared at Zeeran, daring him to disobey.

Zeeran scoffed. "Whatever you say."

Eramus waved his hands, forming a gigantic dome in front of him. In seconds, a wave of blue light crashed into it, pushing him back a few steps. He breathed hard, but the shield held. Morzaun clapped from a few feet away. "Well done! Not bad at all for your first defense."

The encouragement Morzaun offered apparently irked Zeeran, enough so that the line of magical energy grew stronger. Eramus struggled to maintain his spell, the force of Zeeran's attack eating through his magic. He groaned, and his shield dissipated, allowing the light to smash into him. Once again, Eramus gasped from the ground.

"Zeeran! I told you that was enough!"

Morzaun started for the man, but Eramus wasn't about to let him fight his battles. Coughing, he pushed himself to his feet and fired the *impetras*, or as close to it as he could muster, right back. Blue light flowed past Morzaun and struck Zeeran at the waist, throwing him to the ground.

For the briefest moment, a smile washed over Morzaun's face. Zeeran clambered to his feet and conjured his blue aura, ready to retaliate. Eramus summoned his shield and closed his eyes, bracing himself for the attack he was sure his magic couldn't withstand.

When it didn't come, he squinted just enough to glimpse Zeeran's form. His aura had vanished, and he stared across the meadow. Eramus followed his gaze. Evree was heading right for them.

Morzaun's face fell when she stopped a few feet from Eramus. "Hello," she said. Her voice sounded cheery, but he could tell by the way her eyes darted to the two men that she was nervous. "I'm sorry for interrupting your training, but I was hoping I might to steal you for the afternoon?" She leaned closer, whispering. "Since my uncle is officially out of town."

"We *do* have some unfinished business to attend to, don't we?" Eramus smiled, and Evree mirrored it.

"Eramus's training is of the greatest importance," said Morzaun, his mouth pulling into a deep frown. "I'm afraid I insist he stays."

Eramus clenched his fists. Who was Morzaun to dictate his afternoon? "I will stay...but with Evree. I think I've had quite enough training for one day."

Morzaun's brows tightened even more, and Zeeran wrapped his hands around his waist, his bellowing laughter flooding the meadow. "Looks like he'd rather spend time with her than you," he said between gasps. "Not that I can blame him."

Zeeran winked at Evree, and she ducked behind Eramus. A monster of protectiveness gripped him. "Leave her alone."

His cousin held up his hands. "Not to worry, Eramus. I've no interest in your friend."

Morzaun's tone fell over them, harsh and cold. "Leave, Zeeran."

The laughter disappeared from Zeeran's face. He tilted his

head, and a loud crack followed. Words flowed from his lips, a language Eramus didn't understand, and blue light engulfed his body until he vanished.

"I'd like a word with you before I go," said Morzaun.

His dark eyes landed on Evree, and Eramus's stomach flipped. His mind screamed for him to run, to take Evree as far away as possible. But he refused the mark of a coward. He would defend her with his magic, with his life, if necessary.

Eramus bent towards her ear. "Wait here."

She nodded and wrapped her trembling arms around her midsection before he walked away. Evree had never trusted Morzaun, and Zeeran's presence certainly hadn't helped the situation. The more time Eramus spent around Morzaun, the more he believed she was right in her distrust. Morzaun was hiding something, and he would find out what.

Eramus followed him to the tree line, into the shaded area where the air was cooler. Here, where the thick treetops blocked the sunlight, Morzaun's dark eyes matched the shadows.

"What did you wish to discuss?" asked Eramus.

"Nothing. I wish to leave you with a warning." He pointed towards the meadow where Evree stood, her face lifted towards the sun. "She is a distraction, Eramus, and if you do not rid yourself of it, you will regret it."

"Evree is not a distraction. I care for her, and she has done nothing but defend me."

Morzaun scoffed. "Care for her? I believe your affection runs far deeper than that. Love is a weakness, Eramus. The people of

Virgamor will never see us as anything more than evil, as monsters of destruction. King Delran will come for you. Focus is what you need, not some frivolous relationship that will keep you from what's important."

Eramus scowled. "Love is not a weakness. You, yourself, said my father left me and my mother to protect us. He loved her; I know he did. And by the way she spoke of him in my dreams, she loved him too."

Morzaun's expression softened. "They did love each other...and look where that got them. Sytal murdered your mother, and the army of Izarden has hunted your father for the last decade. Think logically, Eramus. Until we accept our destiny and take control, we cannot afford distractions."

He turned and walked a few paces before his body began to disappear. "I'll return in a few days. We'll continue your training then."

In seconds, he vanished. Eramus remained frozen, Morzaun's words echoing across his mind.

Accept our destiny and take control.

His chest tightened. Whatever the man meant by that, Eramus wanted no part in it.

CHAPTER TWELVE
Kissing, Seen

Evree's face contorted as he approached. She averted her eyes, staring down at the flowers at her feet. Eramus touched her arm. "Are you all right?"

She nodded, but her focus remained on the ground. "Morzaun did not like me stealing you away. He looked rather angry with you."

"Don't concern yourself with him. It was my choice to end training. I'm glad you came."

A coy smile stole over her expression as her gaze lifted to meet his eyes. "Were you? I can't fathom why that might be."

He wrapped his fingers around her hand and pulled her

towards the shadows at the tree line. Now that waves of blue magic no longer flowed across the plain, the meadow was peaceful. Several birds chirped noisily as they flew between the branches of the oaks and pines, and a squirrel darted up the knotted side of one particularly old tree.

Eramus plopped down on the ground, wincing a little. Zeeran's attacks had left his rear sore, adding to his collection of injuries for the day. His head throbbed less now, but his upper lip felt larger than normal. He wondered if the swelling was as noticeable as it felt.

Evree plucked a few blades of grass and sighed. "Are you going to tell me what happened this morning?"

A loaded question. Plenty had happened since he'd finished at the bakery. He wasn't sure which part Evree referred to, nor how much he was ready to divulge. "To what are you referring? I've had the most relaxing, normal morning of my entire life."

She scowled and whacked his arm. "I don't believe that for one second. Nothing about your life is normal now that you revealed your secret."

He couldn't deny that, even if he wished it weren't true.

Evree turned and leaned toward him, her shoulder brushing against his arm. His heart took off like a wagon on a steep slope, and Eramus was fairly certain there was a cliff waiting at the bottom. Moments like this never went smoothly for him.

She lifted her hand to his face, gently inspecting his puffy lip. Her warm touch sent chills through his body. She smelled like lavender again.

"How did you get this," she whispered, her breath brushing

across his skin.

Guess that meant the swelling was obvious.

"Your uncle left me a parting gift."

Her brows drew tight, but her fingers lingered on his face. They moved across his cheek, and he was suddenly conscious of the hair he'd continued to neglect. Inara had given up with her chiding reminders, and the stubble had grown into a thick beard.

"I'm sorry. You didn't deserve that."

No, he didn't, but a little pain was worth it to have her soft fingers trailing over his skin. Of course, he couldn't admit to that out loud.

Her hand dropped slowly to her lap, and Eramus had to restrain himself from chasing after it. "Can magic...can you use it to heal injuries?" she asked.

Eramus ran his fingers through his hair. A good question, and one he didn't have an answer for. "I imagine it's possible, but I've never used such a spell, nor has anyone taught me one." And now that Evree had mentioned it, he would be sure to ask. A healing spell would come in handy, especially if things with Arnan continued.

She plucked more grass, biting her lip. "Perhaps Morzaun could teach you."

Her words came with reluctance. He knew Evree was suspicious of the man, and after his discussion with him today, Eramus was close to joining her. "Perhaps, but he isn't the only person I can ask."

Her head jerked toward him, eyes wide with bewilderment.

"What do you mean?"

"It seems I'm not the only one in my family who can wield magic."

Evree's hand shot to her mouth, covering her gasp. "You've learned who your family is?"

He nodded. "A few of them have invaded my house, in fact."

"You're saying there are more people in the village with magical powers?" Her eyes went wide, and she shook her head. "Oh, my uncle will not like this."

"He needn't know. They aren't here to stay. They've come to take me home with them."

Her face paled. "You're...leaving?"

Eramus chewed his cheek. "I haven't decided yet."

Evree looked away from him, her hair falling over her face and shielding her from his view. Her words came out choked. "I know Arnan...the way he's treated you...but I don't want you to go."

Eramus took her hand and pressed it against his chest. She turned to face him, tears streaking across her cheeks. He wiped them away with his thumb. "It's not your uncle, Evree."

He needed her to understand. Eramus disclosed everything, starting with his visions of the past and filling in the details with Morzaun's information. He told her about Yelene and Aldeth, about the Virgàm and the three magical abilities. Evree listened quietly through it all, her tears drying as the sun moved overhead, piercing through the shadows.

"King Delran is out for blood...my blood," said Eramus. "I don't want to leave, but I fear staying will put everyone here in danger. I couldn't live with myself if something happened to the people I care about because of me."

"I understand, but how do you know the king won't follow you? How do you know Verascene is any safer?"

Their hands rested on the ground, and he took to playing with her fingers. "Verascene is nearly impossible to navigate around, let alone land an army on. Delran would sentence his men to death if he attempted such a thing. Even if he succeeded, I would have my aunt and uncle, two experienced magic wielders."

She sighed. "You've only just met. How do you know you can trust them?"

"I don't, but I would much rather take that risk than put our people in jeopardy."

Evree blinked rapidly to contain her tears. "I know it's logical, but..." She wiped her face and jutted her chin towards the meadow. "Perhaps I can help you make your decision."

"Your advice is always welcome."

She turned her whole body towards him and sent his pulse into a frantic gallop when she leaned closer. "Advice was not my intention."

Her lips pressed gently to his. He lost all sense of his surroundings, and time seemed an irrelevant notion. Each breath filled his nostrils with the scent of lavender. Each kiss drew him in deeper. Evree's hands found his chest, gripping his shirt and pulling him closer. One of his hands moved to her nape, his fingers weaving through strands of golden hair, while the other rested on her waist. Warmth flooded over every inch of his body. His kisses deepened with the sensation, brushing over her lips until she pulled away.

She rested her forehead against his, her breathing heavy. "It's selfish," she whispered. "Me trying to convince you to stay. But I don't want to lose you, Eramus."

He chuckled. "Is that what all this was about? Convincing me to stay?"

Evree smiled and softly kissed him again. "I'll only confess if it's working."

"I assure you, it's working exceptionally well."

She giggled and brushed her nose against his. "Do you require more convincing, or was that enough?"

He cleared his throat. "More. Most assuredly."

Evree pulled away and rose, tilting her head to one side as a smug smile stretched across her lips...her perfect, beautiful lips that he had just kissed. "Then perhaps you might consider meeting me here tomorrow? I can convince you more thoroughly then."

As if he could say no to that. "I'll not sleep tonight looking forward to tomorrow."

She lifted her chin and gathered her skirts. "Goodnight, Eramus."

"Goodnight, Evree."

He stayed on the grass, watching her glide across the meadow and disappear out of sight. The sun had ducked behind the mountains by the time he pulled himself to his feet. He needed to focus on making a decision, but his mind kept settling on Evree. Her company filled him with warmth, and her kisses...well, he wasn't sure a word existed for how *those* made him feel.

Eramus stopped outside his cottage. Night had fully descended upon the village, and Inara was certain to chide him for returning home so late. It took him several minutes to wipe the giddy smile off his face. The last thing he wanted was to walk in there wearing *that.*

He shuddered. No one needed to know about that kiss.

When he entered the cottage, Inara was busy at the washbasin, while Yelene and Aldeth sat at the table. All three of them looked at him when he closed the door.

"Where have you been!" Inara ran towards him, her eyes darting from his head to his boots, as though searching for evidence of an excuse. "You realize how late it is, don't you? Had me in an awful dither. Reckless, foolhardy..."

Eramus kissed her on the cheek. "Forgive me, Mother. I didn't mean to make you worry."

She folded her arms and scoffed. "Well, go sit down! Your dinner's cold, but it's your own fault."

He chuckled as she flitted away, muttering indiscernible words. Sitting down at the table, he noticed Aldeth's hand gently placed on his wife's shoulder, his eyes full of concern. Yelene, on the other hand, beamed at him. "Good evening, Eramus."

"Good evening."

"Certainly is." Her lips pinched together as though she were attempting to contain excitement; for what, he didn't know.

Awkward silence ensued. Eramus took a bite of his cold potatoes. Yelene's intense gaze remained fixated on him, and he shifted under her stare.

"Are you certain you don't wish to rest, dear?" asked Aldeth.

Yelene swatted his shoulder. "Oh, will you stop it! This isn't my first vision. I'm just fine."

Eramus looked up. "Vision?"

Aldeth nodded. "She had one about an hour ago. Visions eat up a great deal of energy, causing her to pass out if they are long enough."

"I told you, Aldeth. I'm just fine." She leaned forward, whispering, though it wasn't enough to conceal her words from her husband. "He worries too much. I'm not some fragile old woman. At least not yet."

She winked, and Aldeth rolled his eyes. "Regardless, it wouldn't hurt for you to rest. And I only worry because I love you, so you'll just have to deal with it."

The two exchanged smiles and adoring eyes. Eramus looked away, feeling as though he were intruding on an unspoken conversation happening between them.

"What did you see in your vision," he asked when the silence grew too much to bear.

Yelene smirked. "Oh, nothing of consequence."

Eramus narrowed his eyes. "Nothing of consequence?" He didn't bother to hide his skepticism. Why did it always feel as though people were hiding things from him?

She nodded and hummed an "umm, humm."

Annoying. Eramus planted his chin on his fist. "I don't believe you. Tell me what you saw, and I'll decide for myself."

Yelene bit her lip. "You really don't want me to say it, Eramus."

"Actually, I really do."

Aldeth leaned back in his chair, his brows at the top of his forehead. "You may want to rethink this."

Eramus ignored him, keeping his focus on his aunt.

She sighed. "Very well. First, she's quite a beautiful young lady, and I'm over the moon for you. I can see how happy the two of you make each other."

Eramus's blood ran cold. "I...you what?"

"I'm happy for you, and I understand why deciding whether to leave is so difficult. And after a kiss like that—"

"What kiss?" Inara had appeared at Yelene's side out of nowhere. She bounced on her feet, waiting for an answer.

"Eramus kissed a pretty young lady in the meadow," answered Yelene. "You'll have to ask him for her name. I didn't catch it in my vision."

Inara's mouth hung open, and her eyes danced with excitement. "Eramus! Did you kiss Evree?"

His life held no mercy. Eramus planted his face in his palms and groaned. So much for keeping it a secret.

"I warned you," muttered Aldeth, half chuckling.

"Why in Virgamor would you have a vision about me kissing Evree?" Eramus asked, daring to meet their exuberant expressions. "What purpose could that possibly serve?"

Yelene shrugged. "I don't know. My visions come and go as they please. I have no control over them."

Convenient.

Eramus buried his face again.

"Oh, I'm so happy," said his mother. "He's had an affection for her for a long time. Don't you think they make the cutest couple?"

"Completely adorable," agreed Yelene.

Was this really happening? This nightmare felt worse than the sinking ship that often plagued his dreams. In fact, sinking into oblivion accurately described the way his stomach felt right now.

Eramus pursed his lips and stood. "I think I'll just go to bed now."

He ignored their protests and practically ran to his room. The thin wall wasn't enough to drown out the excited female voices on the other side. He'd never hear the end of this. Of that, he was certain.

CHAPTER THIRTEEN
Family Affairs

Evree's arm wrapped around his. The expressions they passed on their walk through the village varied between knowing smiles and complete disgust. While Eramus had grown accustomed to the mixture of reactions, he worried about the beautiful girl at his side. He covered her hand with his own. Evree beamed up at him, and Eramus returned a half-hearted smile.

"What's the matter?" she asked, frowning.

Blast.

He couldn't hide things from her, no matter how hard he tried.

"Are you sure you're all right with this? With...us?" His eyes darted to the two old ladies outside the cottage a few yards ahead. They leaned close to each other, whispering with wrinkled foreheads.

Evree pulled him to a stop and gave him a pointed look. "I have no reason not to be anything but perfectly content, especially after our time in the meadow this morning."

His lips curled into a wide grin. "Our time in the meadow left you content, did it?"

Her cheeks turned a bright red, and she averted her gaze. It wasn't often that Evree blushed, and Eramus couldn't help but enjoy it when she did. If their first kiss had elicited warmth and desire, the second was nothing short of magical.

Magic. His power. It was the reason he was worried in the first place.

"Evree, I know you care for me, but..." He sighed, glancing at the two women again, who watched them with intense disdain. "People treat me differently now that they know my secret, and they will not see you the same, either. This is not an easy burden to bear, and I don't want you to feel weighted by prejudice."

She slid her hand down his arm until it met his, interlocking their fingers. "Burdens are easier to carry when you don't bear them alone. Whatever we may face, we can do so together. My fear of losing you is far greater than my fear of what people will think."

Evree turned and tugged him further down the dirt path. "The first is a fear you could alleviate if you would promise to stay."

Eramus chewed his cheek. She had asked him first thing this morning about his decision, as had his aunt, uncle, and Inara. But he had no answer for them. He knew he should leave. Staying only put everyone in danger, but Evree's convincing kisses did nothing to encourage him to make the unselfish choice.

"I can't make you that promise, as much as I want to."

Her fingers tightened between his. "I know. When will your family leave?"

"As soon as I decide." He released a long sigh. "Time is of the essence, or so they keep reminding me. For all we know, King Delran is already on his way."

They stopped outside of Evree's home. She glanced up at him with glazed eyes. "If you can't promise you'll stay, at least promise you won't leave without saying goodbye."

Eramus tucked a strand of her golden hair behind her ear. "I promise."

The cottage door swung open, and when Kieran's stony expression fell on Eramus, he tensed. Evree giggled and placed a kiss on his cheek. Kieran's gaze moved skyward, and he folded his arms.

"I'll see you tomorrow," she said, slipping past her father and into the cottage.

Kieran closed the door behind her, and Eramus's heart sped into chaos. "I wanted to speak with you," Kieran said, taking a few steps closer.

Eramus swallowed hard. What did Kieran want with him? Was he going to deny him the courtship of his daughter? Had Arnan finally convinced him against it?

"I wanted to talk to you about Arnan," he continued.

Eramus's stomach rolled, but he kept his tone even. "What about him?"

Kieran sighed. "Evree told me how he's treated you since...well, you know. I believe he feels threatened by your gift."

"Why?" said Eramus, shaking his head. "I've no interest in taking his position. I'm no leader, nor do I wish to be."

"I realize that, and I hope Arnan will eventually, as well. I don't condone his behavior. This misplaced prejudice against you evades justice and reason. If his aggression persists, I'll put him in his place. I want you to keep me informed when he's out of line."

Keep him informed? No way that was happening. The last thing he needed was someone fighting his battles for him. "Kieran, I appreciate your concern, but I can handle Arnan on my own. Whatever grudge he holds against me will pass once he realizes I've no desire to take his place."

Kieran scoffed. "I think you underestimate my brother." He paused for a moment, his mouth twitching to accompany the glisten in his eyes. "Then again, I believe my brother underestimates you. Punching you in the face wasn't the wisest decision. With your power, you could take him with the wave of your hand."

"I don't want to fight Arnan. I don't want to fight anyone."

Kieran's mouth flattened into a straight line, and his gaze grew glassy. Silence stole over them for several moments as Kieran sank into some trance-like state. "We all have to fight sometimes," he said finally. "Life often requires more of us than we believe we can give. Whether fighting is what you want or not, prepare yourself for it. If not for yourself, then for those you care about."

The words struck Eramus's heart. Everyone in the village knew of Kieran's misfortunes. He and his wife had made the trip to Olgetha to deliver the harvest to the port. Once they exchanged the goods, they began their return trip, only for a band of highwaymen to rob them of the profits. Kieran's wife had refused to comply with their demands. A fight ensued, and three people lost their lives, hers included.

According to Eramus's mother, Kieran was never the same after the incident. He blamed himself and vowed to never leave their small village again. Neither he nor Evree ever made the journey to Olgetha, despite Evree's persistent pleas to do so. She was young when her mother died, too young to understand or remember the perils such a journey could bring.

Kieran's hand pressed on Eramus's shoulder. "I'm not telling you to fight my brother, but I can't promise it won't come to that. Arnan is...stubborn." He cleared his throat. "A family trait, I'm told."

Eramus contained his laughter, but just barely. "Not the worst trait to have. Evree has always been one to stand up for what she believes in. I think that's an admirable quality."

The grin that spread across Kieran's face made Eramus's stomach lurch. "Undoubtedly not the only admirable quality you see in her." One of his brows lifted. "I'm well aware of how much time you've spent together in the meadow. If you were anyone less respectable, I might have given you a bruised face myself."

"I'm motivated to remain respectable."

Kieran laughed and slapped Eramus's shoulder. "Good man. Now, I've got work to do. Keep yourself out of trouble."

"I'll do my best."

Making his way to his cottage, an overwhelming warmth swept over him. After Eramus revealed his power, he never expected his people to trust him so quickly. He never expected Kieran to grant him permission to court Evree. Despite his life being upturned, despite how Arnan treated him, Eramus was grateful the consequences were not worse.

Eramus tugged on the cottage door. His mother scampered across the room to greet him, and Yelene gave him a small wave from the wooden table. A book and inkwell lay in front of her. Eramus strode to her side and examined the odd symbols smeared across the parchment.

"What's this?" he asked, leaning forward to see over Yelene's shoulder.

"Our spell book," she replied cheerily. "I note all the spells we learn so we have a record."

His brows tightened as his eyes traced the strange shapes and squiggles. "You can read that?"

Yelene giggled. "Yes. Someone wrote symbols like this on the walls of the cavern where we found the Virgàm. When we first moved to Verascene, I began hearing a voice inside my head. It taught me the language and instructed me to compile our spells into this book."

She snapped it closed, bringing the cover into his view. Etched into the leather were several symbols, each a different color. A large blue circle encompassed a green triangle and a purple crescent moon. A golden eye filled the center, its eerie gaze making his heart race.

"These symbols...the colors, do they represent the abilities Aldeth spoke of?"

"That's correct." Aldeth's voice sounded from behind them. The man joined his wife at the table and placed a soft kiss on her cheek. Yelene smiled warmly at him, exchanging more unspoken words with just their eyes. Something about knowing his aunt and uncle loved one another flooded him with warmth.

"These symbols represent the three abilities of magic," said Aldeth, tapping his finger on each one. "The details came to Yelene through visions."

Eramus studied the book cover for several moments. "But what of this golden eye in the center? You never mentioned a fourth ability?"

Morzaun had mentioned four gems when he spoke of the Virgàm. That couldn't be a coincidence.

Yelene sighed. "The eye is still a mystery, I'm afraid. I've yet to understand what it means or its significance. I suppose we shall in time."

As intriguing as the book was, Eramus had more pressing questions. He turned to Aldeth and cleared his throat. What was he to call the man? Uncle? Aldeth? The uncertainty made him squirm.

"Aldeth," he said, deciding the more formal option was best. "I wonder if I might...would you..." Eramus ran his fingers through his hair. Why was it so difficult to ask the man for assistance? He was family, and Eramus no longer distrusted either of them. Still, he had managed this long without help, and his pride made him hesitate.

"I was wondering if there was a spell for healing, and if so, whether you would teach it to me?" The words came out rushed. Eramus averted his eyes, choosing to stare at the spell book rather than face his uncle.

Aldeth's tone was soft, as was his smile. "Of course I would teach you." He tapped his finger against his nose and grinned. "A healing spell would prove quite useful for you, I think. Next time you take a punch, you can clean yourself up in a matter of seconds. Save your mother the heartache."

Eramus laughed and glanced over to where Inara chopped vegetables for their evening meal. Aldeth was right; a healing spell would benefit them both.

Aldeth rose from his chair beside Yelene and moved to Eramus's side of the table. He rolled up his sleeves. "Without an actual injury to heal, it's a little complicated to learn, but I can at least teach you the incantation. However, I wholeheartedly advise against you getting hurt just to practice using it."

"Fair enough," said Eramus. "Better to have some experience than none at all."

Another smile washed across Aldeth's face. "Right."

His uncle taught him strange words that twisted his tongue into unforgiving knots, and after several attempts, Eramus conjured his aura to accompany them. He had no way of knowing if the spell would heal anything, but having it in his arsenal of magic comforted him. If things with Arnan continued, self healing would come in handy.

Eramus scratched at the wooden table once the lesson was over.

He still had so many questions, but no way to ask them without revealing he knew of Morzaun and Zeeran. Yelene and Aldeth likely already suspected *something*, what with his knowledge of the Virgàm and lack of surprise regarding his father's quarrel with the king. How would they respond if they knew he was in contact with them? Although he wasn't aware of any details regarding their relationship, he sensed there was some discord.

Aldeth chuckled, seeming to sense his thoughts. "Is there more you wished to ask me? Or perhaps spells you wished to learn?"

"I know my magic came from my father," he started with some hesitation. Aldeth's brows raised high on his forehead, but he said nothing. "Is he a Protesta? Like me?"

What ability his father possessed didn't really matter. It was Eramus's roundabout way of asking a question. He had assumed that his magic and, specifically, his ability passed to him from his father, but meeting Zeeran made him question the notion. Aldeth was an Elementalist and Yelene a Seer. Why, then, was Zeeran's aura blue like his own?

Aldeth scratched the back of his head. "Yes, your father was a Protesta."

Was? Aldeth and Yelene had spoken as though his father was alive, and Morzaun had stated as much, but his uncle's phrasing left him confused. He had little time to dwell on the question as Aldeth continued.

"We pass on our capability to use magic, but not necessarily our abilities. Think of it as random, the roll of a die. For example, Yelene and I have three children. Ladisias is an Elementalist, like me. Zeeran is a Protesta, and Feya is a Seer. If you decide to come back to Verascene with us, you'll get to meet your cousins. I know Ladisias, especially, is hoping you will."

Eramus bit his lip. "And Zeeran and Feya? Do they live on Verascene with you as well?"

There was no mistaking the shift in Aldeth's expression. His eyes filled with sadness, and guilt struck Eramus for asking. He knew Zeeran did not reside with his family, and his curiosity desperately wanted to know why.

When Aldeth remained quiet, Yelene answered for him, her voice filled with the same sorrow. "Feya and her husband live with us, but I'm afraid Zeeran has chosen a different path."

Pulling himself from his trance, Aldeth leaned forward and propped his chin with his fist. "There is something you must understand, Eramus. Not everyone who possesses magic uses their power for good. There are some who believe we are superior, that we should rule over Virgamor solely because of our magic, even if it means the loss of innocent lives."

"And Zeeran...is that what he believes?"

"I'm afraid he might," said Aldeth. "I only hope he finds his way home."

No matter how much he wanted to press for more answers, Eramus couldn't bring himself to do so. The pain etched across Aldeth's face was more than he could bear. Whatever had caused Zeeran to stray from his family weighed heavily on his aunt and uncle, and Eramus wondered if Morzaun had played a role in his cousin's dissent.

A light tap sounded from the door. Inara rushed to answer its plea. When the door swung open, a young man Eramus recognized stood in the frame. His expression was tight, just like the day Eramus revealed his power.

"Kieran has called a meeting," the young man said. "He's asked everyone to come."

CHAPTER FOURTEEN
Foreign Threats

The young man's eyes darted from Inara to Eramus, widening as they finally landed on Yelene and Aldeth. Yelene leapt from her chair, taking his confusion as the perfect moment to introduce herself.

"Hello," she said, extending her hand towards him. "My name is Yelene, and that"—she pointed to Aldeth, who offered a small, reluctant smile—"is my husband, Aldeth. We're here visiting Eramus. I'm sure you know him."

The man's gaze fixated on Eramus, and his throat bobbed with a large swallow. "Y-yes. I-I know Eramus."

Of course he did. Everyone knew everyone in their tiny village, and after revealing to the world he could use magic, no one would forget him. Eramus could see the poor fellow trembling all the way from his spot at the table. He would probably flee faster than a chicken in a fox den if he knew Yelene and Aldeth could also wield magic.

Eramus stood and gave the man a slight bow. "Cavell, how are you this evening?"

Cavell relaxed a little. "Fine...I think."

Inara planted her hands on her hips and scowled. "A meeting? You said Kieran has called for one. What about?"

Cavell shrugged. "Sorry, Ma'am, but I don't have a clue. He just said I was to round everyone up. Sounded pretty on edge. 'Course, Kieran usually sounds that way."

No one could argue against that. Kieran and Arnan were much alike, both as firm and serious as a stone wall. But one thing was certain, Kieran would not have called a meeting unless it was important. Unlike Arnan, he preferred to keep to himself, not parade around as leader.

"Very well," said Eramus. "Thank you for informing us, Cavell."

Cavell bowed and ducked out of the cottage without so much as a second glance. Eramus's stomach twisted with guilt at man's nervousness in his presence, but there was little he could do about it.

Inara placed her palm against her chest. "Oh, dear. What do you suppose this is all about? I didn't particularly enjoy the last meeting."

Eramus chuckled. "I can't imagine why."

She chided him with her eyes. "I suppose we should go find out. See what all the fuss is about."

Yelene started for the door, but both Eramus and Aldeth called after her.

—"Wait!"

—"Don't go!"

She tossed them each a scowl and folded her arms. "You don't think I'm going to just stay here?"

Eramus turned to Aldeth, pleading without words. Aldeth grudgingly rose and moved to Yelene's side. "We need to stay here. Eramus is under enough scrutiny as it is. Having strangers accompany him will only make his people more anxious."

The wrinkles on her forehead deepened. "Do his *people* have a problem with family visiting him? That's absurd."

Aldeth took her face between his hands and smiled. "And how are we to explain how we came to find him after all these years? You know they will ask questions. What if you have a vision whilst we are there? How do you think they might respond to that?"

Yelene pursed her lips. "You could just tell them I passed out? How are they to know any different?"

"And if you scream or shout, as you often do? They may think you're insane."

"So? You know I'm not."

Aldeth chuckled and pressed his forehead to hers. "Do I?"

Yelene opened her mouth to rebuff, but Aldeth captured her breath with a quick kiss. "We'll wait here, and Eramus can tell us about it when he returns. That way, no one will think you're insane, except perhaps me."

She narrowed her eyes. "You are fortunate my affection for you runs so deep; otherwise I might just use my magic on you."

Aldeth's smile stretched from one side of his face to the other. "You did, long before we had powers, love."

"All right," said Eramus after clearing his throat. "I think I'll leave now."

He appreciated that his aunt and uncle loved each other, but the whole situation was growing awkward. They could exchange all the mushy sentiments they wanted once he and his mother left.

Inara walked beside him down the dirt path leading out of the village. A crowd gathered at the edge of the meadow, and Kieran stood at the front. Eramus made his way forward and stopped at Evree's side.

"Evree, what's going on?" he asked, touching her arm.

She shook her head. "I'm not sure. Papa came home so distressed. Would barely speak to me." She shifted closer and wrapped her hand around his arm. "I'm worried about him. Arnan usually handles these sorts of things."

Eramus glanced at Kieran. Dark circles rested beneath his eyes and deep lines etched above his brows. He looked nothing like he had during their discussion earlier that morning. Whatever caused him to call this meeting burdened him with concern.

"I don't think I've seen him this distraught in a long time," said Inara. "This must be serious."

Eramus pointed toward Kieran, who was holding his hands out

in front of him to silence the crowd. "We're about to find out."

Whispers dulled to silence as Kieran began. "I appreciate everyone gathering so quickly, and I hope you'll forgive my interruption, but there is some pressing news I think everyone should be aware of."

Kieran gestured to a man standing a few feet away, coaxing him forward. He wasn't from the village, nor was he someone Eramus recognized, and he seemed hesitant to put himself on display. Eramus couldn't blame him. He knew how uncomfortable that was.

"This is Lamaus," said Kieran. "He is from a village south of here and has come to warn us."

Murmurs echoed through the crowd. Kieran raised his hands, reigning in the noise without words. He nodded to Lamaus, and the man twisted a brown beret restlessly in his hands. "Mercenaries plundered my village three days ago. Our leader sent me to warn as many other villages as I could before they met the same fate. These men set fire to our homes and stole our most valuable possessions. They also injured several people."

"Are they headed in our direction?" asked an elderly woman with silver hair piled on top of her head.

Lamaus nodded and bunched the beret in his fist. "I'm afraid they are headed north, camped just a few miles from here."

"How many?" asked another man. "If we take them by surprise, we can keep our families safe!"

"At least a hundred," answered Lamaus. "I don't recommend making an attack on them. They seemed well trained, and your small numbers wouldn't stand a chance. Best you can do is prepare yourselves, perhaps even leave for the time being."

"Leave!" someone shouted. "I will not leave my home. I will defend it!"

The crowd grew into an uproar. Arguments ensued, debating whether leaving or standing firm was the best option.

"Enough!" Kieran shouted over them. "I know the information leaves us with a tough decision, but that is no reason to fight amongst ourselves. None of us want to abandon our homes, even if it is for a short time, but leaving may be the safest option."

Eramus's heart pounded hard against his ribs. Even if his people left, who was to say the mercenaries wouldn't follow. Besides, he couldn't stand the idea of giving up, not when it risked losing so much. His people lived simple lives, and if the mercenaries burned the village to the ground, they would have nothing.

"We don't have to leave," said Eramus, drawing every pair of horrified eyes towards him. "We can stand against them."

Inara grabbed his arm, her eyes wide. "What are you saying! You better not be suggesting what I think you are!"

Kieran folded his arms. "I won't ask you to put yourself at risk for us. Even with your abilities—"

"With my abilities, I can defend everyone here without us having to abandon our homes. I am more than capable of this task." At least, he thought so. Sure his training with Zeeran hadn't gone well, but his cousin had magic. The mercenaries did not.

Kieran shook his head. "It's still dangerous. I won't ask you to do this."

"You don't have to ask. This is my home. I won't stand idly by while some thugs threaten everything I care about." Eramus pushed through the crowd and stopped in front of Kieran. "Please. What is the point of possessing this gift if I cannot use it for good. I want to help my people. It's all I've *ever* wanted."

Kieran studied him, his expression tight. This was the opportunity Eramus needed to prove himself. If he could show the villagers that he desired to protect them, perhaps he could earn back their trust. Even if he decided to leave with Aldeth and Yelene, he preferred to go knowing his people did not hate and despise him.

Kieran's expression softened. "Then we must thank you for offering so much, Eramus. You are a brave man, and no one can question your honor." His mouth lifted just enough for Eramus to notice. Kieran gave him a small nod and turned his attention back to the crowd.

"Eramus has graciously offered to defend us. If we are to protect our village, then we need volunteers to stand watch. Perhaps these mercenaries will return home, but until they have vacated the area, we must remain vigilant. Who else is up for the task?"

A dozen hands shot skyward in seconds. A wave of relief washed over Eramus. If he could help his village...if he could protect them from the mercenaries, then maybe he would find his place again. Maybe he would even have the confidence to face King Delran.

Lamaus was staring at him with raised brows, complete confusion etched across his face. "Forgive me, but I must take my leave. I hope for your success, but I must inform as many villages as I can."

Kieran extended his hand. "Thank you. We owe you a great deal for warning us. Best of luck."

Lamaus gave Kieran's hand a firm shake before disappearing into the shadows of the forest. The sun lay low on the horizon now, and if what the man said was true, the mercenaries would likely begin their assault at first light. That gave them little time to prepare.

"Very well," said Kieran. "We will discuss the best places to establish posts, taking shifts starting tonight. With enough warning, we can stop them before they even set foot in the village. If the volunteers will join me, we can create a plan. I encourage the rest of you to return home. For your safety, I ask you not to stray from the village until we resolve this matter."

Eramus stared out over the crowd as the people dispersed. Inara and Evree rushed towards him. His mother's hand whacked his shoulder, making him flinch.

"What were you thinking!" said Inara. "Just because you have magic doesn't mean you need to put yourself in danger. You're not invincible. This is absolutely preposterous." She placed her hands on her hips and turned to Kieran. "Tell him this is ridiculous. We should go somewhere safe, not risk our lives."

Kieran exchanged a glance with him. "I'm sorry, Inara, but Eramus is our best chance at stopping them before the worst can happen. Besides, it is not my place to tell him what he can and cannot do."

"Well, make it your place! Arnan isn't here. Everyone knows you should be the one leading our people, not him. Now is the perfect time for you to step into a role that suits you better than farming."

Kieran's eyes danced with mirth, and a small smile tugged at his lips. "I'm quite content with my work in the fields, Inara. I have no desire for a position of leadership, but I will take charge in my brother's absence. Eramus is old enough to make his own decisions, and I am happy to accept his help."

Inara muttered something inaudible, but her disgruntled expression gave her opinion without words.

Eramus took her hand with both of his own. "Mother, please. I know you are only worried about me, but this is something that I must do. I refuse to cower when these men threaten our home. Not when I can do something about it."

She sighed, her glossy eyes staring back at him with concern. "All right. Just promise me you'll be careful. If something happened to you—"

"Nothing will happen to me. Or you. Or anyone else."

Inara sniffled and nodded. Evree patted her arm. "Come stay with me tonight. We can fret over them together. At least we can keep each other company."

"That is a splendid idea, Evree," said Kieran. "It will comfort me knowing you are not alone tonight."

His mother passed him one last pleading look. "Company would be nice." She paused, her eyes rounding. "Company. Oh, I must return home first, then I will come to your cottage."

Evree nodded, glancing briefly at Eramus. She was aware his aunt and uncle currently resided in their home. Inara would have to inform them of the situation, but Eramus hoped they would not get involved. The revelation that more magic wielders existed may be too much for his people to handle, and he believed he could deal with the mercenaries on his own. Training with Morzaun and actually being able to practice magic without fear someone would catch him had boosted his confidence significantly. He was stronger, and spells came easier with every incantation he cast.

Eramus kissed Inara's cheek. "Everything will be fine. I promise."

To his surprise, a wide grin commandeered her lips. "Are you going to give Evree a parting kiss as well?"

Heat crept up the back of his neck all the way to his ears. "Mother," he said through gritted teeth.

Inara shrugged. "What? It's not like it would be the first time."

Eramus groaned. He dared to steal a glance at Kieran. The man scowled at him, his stance wide and his arms crossed over his chest.

"I believe that is my cue to leave," said Kieran, but his feet remained firmly in place. "Eramus, you and I will need to have another discussion...soon. Once you're *finished*, please join us so we can prepare."

He marched away, and Eramus's stomach traipsed so wildly he felt nauseous. Why must his mother insist on embarrassing him?

Evree stepped forward and kissed his cheek, flashing him a coy smile. "Be careful. Your mother and I will worry over you all night, so don't do anything too reckless."

She took Inara by the arm, and together they left the soft grass of the meadow and followed the dirt path back to the village.

Orange clouds streaked across the sky as the sun faded behind the mountains. Kieran gave the volunteers instructions, and soon, a plan to thwart the foreign threat was in place. Eramus stared down at his palms, his only weapon to protect everything he held dear. His power had grown with Morzaun's training, but he couldn't help but wonder if his magic was enough.

CHAPTER FIFTEEN
Taken

E ramus kicked at the ground, sending a cloud of dust into the air. His eyes were heavy, but he suspected he wouldn't sleep even if he went home. The night had been long. Hours crept by, and every snapping twig or rustle of leaves sent his heart racing. The mercenaries could attack at any moment, or they may not attack at all. The uncertainty unsettled him, and he wished they would make a move so he could deal with the situation.

The sun had barely peeked over the mountains, slowly chasing away the shadows of night. From where he sat on a fallen tree, he could not see the village or any of the other volunteers who agreed to stand as watchmen. Kieran's plan was simple. He'd positioned half a dozen men around the outskirts of their village. The moment one of them spotted the mercenaries, they were to alert everyone. That's when Eramus would step in. With his abilities, he could take them out before the thugs did any damage. He hoped to chase them off, to scare them into retreating without having to use excessive force. After all, his brief use of magic in the village had scared many of his people, and that was without trying to do so.

With any luck, these men would take one look at his power and run back from whence they came. The last thing he wanted was for his people to sustain injury, nor did he have any desire to hurt the invaders, even if they were here to cause chaos and destruction.

His mind wandered to Evree and his mother. How were they holding up? He imagined Inara pacing the floor, and Evree attempting to calm her. That she had taken it upon herself to offer his mother comfort warmed his soul and only deepened his ever-growing affection for her. He still hadn't determined whether to leave, and the decision grew harder with each passing day...with each moment he spent in her company.

Eramus's heart ached at the idea of never seeing her again. For all his strength and magical power, he wasn't certain he was strong enough to leave Evree behind.

A small, brown squirrel jumped onto the log next to him and wiggled its nose, sniffing the air. The creature held a tiny acorn in its hands and eyed Eramus with curiosity.

"What do you think? Should I stay here, or should I leave?"

The squirrel gave no response beyond a furious flick of its tail. "I know the selfless thing to do is leave," he continued. "But I fear my heart would remain here. Putting my people in danger is selfish, but how does one abandon love? Abandon the potential for happiness? I know Evree cares for me."

He paused, watching the animal scratch at the weathered bark. "Perhaps I should ask her to come with me?"

He'd considered the idea so many times. Evree agreeing to accompany him to Verascene would make his decision easy, but it would also require him to ask for her hand. Eramus knew Evree would accept an offer from him, but how Kieran would respond was another thing entirely. Granting his blessing would mean Evree may never see her father again, a difficult thing for any parent to accept.

A series of loud chirps and squeaks filled the area as the squirrel scratched and shifted manically along the log. After several moments, it darted across the little clearing and clambered up a tall pine, still squeaking loudly.

Did he just get chided by a squirrel? The creature certainly had much to say about the situation, and it was a shame Eramus didn't speak the language. An unbiased opinion could have proved useful. Inara was no help, as she wanted nothing more than to keep him safe, even if it meant never seeing him again, and Evree desperately wanted him to stay. Her kisses alone were nearly enough to make him consider abandoning the idea of leaving altogether.

His mouth lifted without permission. Kissing Evree seemed a pleasant way to spend the evening when all of this was over.

The sound of a snapping branch jerked him out of his thoughts. Eramus stood, watching the forest for any sign of movement as his heart pounded out of control. The rustle of leaves grew closer. In seconds, a familiar figure emerged from two large bushes.

"Eramus," said Cavell between heavy gasps. He bent over, placing his hands on his knees, his chest heaving with his sharp breaths. "You must come back immediately. The mercenaries...they broke through. They attacked the village."

His blood ran cold. Eramus didn't bother to wait for an explanation, bolting towards the village without hesitation. His heart hammered. What would he find when he reached his home? How much damage could the mercenaries have caused before Cavell reached him? Were Evree and his mother safe? He ran faster, branches scratching his skin as he trudged through the thick briers and shrubs. They were all right; they had to be.

Eramus's heart sank into his stomach the moment he left the confines of the forest. Smoke billowed from several cottages, and he could hear cries of anguish echoing in the distance. He ran down the dirt path until he came to a large crowd. Tears streamed across fear-stricken faces. Children clung to their sobbing mothers, and several people lay on the ground with blood-stained clothes.

Ordin leaned against an overturned cart, holding a cloth against his head. Eramus rushed to his side and crouched beside him. "Ordin, are you all right? What happened?"

The man shook his head, refusing to look at him. "They jumped me. Didn't even hear them coming. It was so dark, and there were too many of them to take on by myself." He turned towards Eramus, his eyes glazed. "It's my fault. I didn't get the chance to warn anyone. They knocked me unconscious."

Eramus glanced at the cloth Ordin pressed to the right side of his skull. Blood soaked the piece, and more red liquid dripped past his ear. Ordin's gaze grew distant. His head dipped to one side, and his hand fell to his side. Eramus grabbed Ordin's face, his body trembling. "Ordin! No...Ordin, wake up. Please, wake up!"

A hand touched his shoulder. Aldeth crouched beside them and placed his palm on Ordin's injury. The incantation flowed from his mouth like a melody, and green light surrounded his hand. Ordin's wound became nothing more than a scar.

"He's going to be fine," said Aldeth calmly. "He'll just need some rest."

Eramus stared at him. He was grateful Aldeth stepped in to help Ordin, but the act would have consequences. His eyes darted to the crowd that encompassed them, surprised to find a lack of shocked expressions. Why were the people not in complete panic?

"Aldeth," Eramus said in a whisper. "You shouldn't use your magic in front of everyone. They—"

"Have already seen," interrupted Aldeth, returning his hand to Eramus's shoulder. "When we heard the commotion, Yelene and I didn't wait for an invitation to offer assistance. The mercenaries caused some damage before we arrived, but we chased them off with little effort. Didn't seem too keen to stick around after I gave one of them a face full of boils."

Eramus grimaced. He couldn't blame anyone for that.

"They saved us," came Ordin's low, muttered voice. He opened his eyes and offered them a weak smile. "So, there are more oddballs like you. Good to know. Perhaps I can convince them to work the mill too."

Eramus chuckled. "I'm afraid they aren't here to stay, but that is a discussion for another time. You need to rest." He turned to Aldeth. "Where is Yelene?"

"She went to check on your mother while I helped the injured but hasn't returned. Go check on them. I'll stay here and do what I can."

"Thank you, Aldeth."

Although he had hoped his aunt and uncle would not need to get involved, Eramus was glad they had taken the initiative to help. The mercenaries had thwarted Kieran's plan, and because Eramus had taken a watch post instead of remaining in the village, his people were subject to the invaders' mercy. Thanks to Yelene and Aldeth, the village had sustained only minor damage and the people few injuries. It knotted his stomach to think what would have happened had they not been here.

Eramus rushed to Evree's cottage and knocked on the door. He expected her or Kieran to appear in the frame, but it was Yelene's petite form that stood before him. She brushed her blonde hair from her face, giving the sunlight a chance to reflect off the trail of tears on her cheeks.

"Eramus!" She sprung forward and wrapped him in a warm embrace. "Are you all right?" she asked, pulling away to look him over.

"I'm fine. How is my mother? Evree?"

Her face paled, and she offered no response. "Come inside."

He entered the cottage, immediately catching the sound of angry voices.

"You won't stop me from going!" Kieran shouted, rummaging through a closet near the back of the room. "I'm going after them, whether you like it or not."

"Listen to reason!" came a voice Eramus recognized as Arnan's. "You are one man. You can't possibly contend with so many. Only a fool would think they could take them on their own."

Arnan must have returned late last night or early this morning from Olgetha. Whatever he and Kieran were arguing about had the man flustered, his face as red as a beet.

"I suppose I am a fool, then," said Kieran, pulling what looked like a spear from inside the closet. "But I won't stand here and do nothing. She's my daughter!"

A wave of chills swept over Eramus. His eyes darted frantically around the room. Inara sat at the table, her arms folded and tears streaming down her face. Her shoulders shook with her sobs, and Yelene hovered over her, whispering soft words of comfort.

But where was Evree? The realization that she wasn't among them sent his pulse into a frenzy. "What happened?" he said over the argument across the room. "Where is Evree?"

Kieran and Arnan both turned to face him. Kieran's expression fell, and his sullen eyes made Eramus's stomach lurch into his throat. Arnan wasted no time marching across the room, his hands clenched and his gaze dark.

"You!" He used both hands to shove Eramus several steps backwards. "You have deceived us yet again. There are more people like you! How dare you hide such information from us!"

"That's enough, Arnan!" Kieran shouted, but the effort did little good.

Arnan sneered. "What else are you hiding? What other secrets do you have? Did you ask your friends to come so you could take over?"

Eramus almost snorted. Why Arnan believed he had any interest in "taking over" their little village, he would never understand. The man was losing his sanity over the idea that Eramus wanted to replace him, and he couldn't be further from the truth.

Regardless, now wasn't the time for his pettiness.

"What do you expect? Should I subjugate them to the same prejudice I've experienced the last few weeks? They just protected our people from mercenaries, yet you still think ill of magic." Eramus inched closer to him, jabbing a finger into Arnan's chest. "You think I'm a threat to this village, but it is you who can't see past your own selfish desires. I've done nothing to deserve your deplorable treatment, and I would never put anyone in the same position."

Yelene rushed to his side and gripped his arm. "Stop, please! Both of you! Now is not the time."

Arnan's scowl deepened. "You think they protected everyone? Not quite, Eramus. Perhaps you should ask Kieran if they protected *everyone*. I assure you, he will agree with me this time."

Eramus turned to face Kieran, waiting for his response. Kieran's gaze dropped to the floor and time dragged. When he finally looked up, tears filled his eyes.

"They took her, Eramus. They've taken Evree."

CHAPTER SIXTEEN

Rescue Mission

Time froze, and the room rippled as his focus drew to a point, shadows invading the edges of his vision. Eramus reached for the wall, stumbling sideways until his fingers found something sturdy to cling to. His arms trembled and his legs nearly buckled out from under him.

"Taken?"

The word died on his lips, the air in his lungs becoming stale and forcing him to breathe.

"Yes," muttered Kieran. "They took her before I arrived back at the village. Your aunt and uncle scared them off, but not before they got their hands on Evree."

Eramus's eyes focused, bringing the blurry image of a chair into view. His grip tightened around the top of it. "But...I don't understand. Why would they take her?"

Arnan folded his arms and scoffed. "What difference does it make *why*? Point is she's gone, and going after her is suicide."

Kieran grumbled something inaudible and began rummaging through his things again. Eramus drew a deep breath. This was no time to panic. "The *why* could make all the difference. If they were here to plunder, then why take a hostage? That makes no sense."

Two long strides brought Arnan within a few feet of him. "They're mercenaries. Someone hired them to do a job, and I suspect plundering wasn't it. Taking Evree wasn't a coincidence; she's too close to *you*."

Eramus's clenched his hands. "What exactly are you implying?"

"You know what I'm implying. Our village knew peace for over a century until you came along with your power. Now my niece, who you happen to have an affection for, has been taken by men of the most indecent character. You are responsible for this; I know it."

Heat washed over Eramus. Arnan's words stabbed him like a thick blade. He could argue against him, but truthfully, Arnan could very well be right. Nothing about the situation made sense, and Eramus couldn't help but wonder if responsibility rested on him.

"They took her," Inara's quiet whimper echoed from across the room. "They just...took her."

Yelene grabbed a small blanket and wrapped it around Inara's shoulders before flashing Eramus an expression of concern. He rushed towards the table and crouched in front of them. "Mother, what happened? Tell me everything."

She sniffled when he wrapped his fingers around her hand, and her watery eyes met his. "We heard a commotion outside. Evree went to the window to see what was going on. We could see Aldeth and Yelene using their magic to stop them, and then one entered the cottage. He spotted me first, but I was of no interest to him. The moment he found Evree..." Her voice trailed into sobs, and she buried her face into her palms.

Eramus's stomach rolled. They had targeted Evree specifically from what his mother described. Arnan's assumptions were looking more sound by the second. "Is there anything else? Did he say anything more?"

Inara nodded. "At first, he drew his sword. I thought for certain he was going to...but he didn't. He said something about changing his plans, and that's when he grabbed her. I tried to stop him, but the man was so strong. He threw me to the floor, and by the time I could right myself, he had disappeared." Her voice cracked, a fresh stream of tears flooding her cheeks. "I'm so sorry, Eramus. I'm sorry I couldn't stop him."

He squeezed her hand. "Don't apologize. None of this is your fault. I'm just glad they didn't hurt you."

"It's your son who should apologize," said Arnan. "He may have escaped banishment before, but he won't be so lucky this time. Your defense of him only taints your own reputation."

Inara shuddered, and Eramus stood, facing Arnan with a deep furrow in his forehead. He would own the consequences his power brought on himself, but he wouldn't allow Arnan to speak or treat his mother with the same condescension.

"Leave my mother out of this."

"Or what? You going to use your magic on me? I know you want to...have for a while. I can see it in your eyes. You can't cage a monster forever."

Eramus wanted nothing more than to pummel the man, but he needed to keep his emotions in check. He needed to stay focused, for Evree's sake.

Kieran marched across the room, a large brown sack over his shoulder and a long blade sheathed at his side. Before he could reach the door, Arnan grabbed him by the shoulder and pulled him to a stop.

"Don't be a fool! You can't fight them all yourself!"

Kieran jerked away from him. "I won't ask our people to risk their lives, nor will I give up on my daughter, even if that means facing an army alone."

"You won't be facing them alone," said Eramus, following Kieran to the door. "I'm going with you."

"You're not going anywhere!"

Arnan lunged towards him. Eramus's palms rose in response, a blue light encircling them in seconds. His magic did nothing to deter the man, and when Arnan was a few feet away, Eramus launched a small wave of energy at his chest. He flew across the room and landed on his back with a groan.

"You'll pay for that," Arnan said with a growl. "Accept your banishment."

"I don't care! Banish me! Right now, my only concern is finding Evree." Though his skin prickled with fury, Eramus stepped towards

Arnan and outstretched his hand. "Evree needs our help. Are you coming with us or not?"

For a moment, Arnan stared at Eramus's hand, his brows drawn so tight they almost touched.

"I'm coming," he said finally, slapping away the gesture and rising to his feet. "I will protect my family from the mercenaries *and* from you." He stormed out of the cottage, slamming the door against the inner wall.

Kieran sighed, his expression riddled with an unspoken apology. "Thank you, Eramus." He disappeared in the sunlight that percolated through the door.

Eramus turned around, his gaze settling on his mother and Yelene. "Will you stay with her?" he asked, nodding towards Inara's trembling form.

Yelene rubbed Inara's shoulders, a weak smile pulling at her lips. "Of course." She bit her lip for a moment, her concerns revealing themselves through the deep creases in her forehead. "Are you certain about this? Perhaps Aldeth—"

Eramus shook his head. "He should stay here. We don't know what the mercenaries have planned. They could return, and I would prefer Aldeth to be here just in case. I can handle myself, but my people stand little chance against well-trained men."

Her expression softened as she studied him. "You remind me so much of him...at least who he used to be." Eramus opened his mouth to question her words, but Yelene quickly cut him off as though she'd made a mistake. "Go. Find Evree and promise me you'll be careful. I worked hard to find you, and I can't lose you now that I have."

Though he did not allow his emotions to show, Eramus was grateful for his aunt and uncle. In the short time they had stayed in his home, Eramus had formed a connection with them, and the warmth he experienced in their company could only come from knowing they truly cared about him.

"I promise," he said, moving towards the door. Eramus paused in the cascade of light that fell through the open doorway. "And thank you, Yelene."

He glanced over his shoulder to find a perplexed look on her face. "For what?"

A half smile pulled his lips to one side. "For never giving up on your nephew. For finding me."

Yelene mirrored his sentiments and nodded. As he crossed the threshold of the cottage, a mixture of emotions surged through his body, but despite the chaos of his racing mind, one thing became clear—Verascene would be his new home.

* * *

"It's the most logical plan," said Eramus, trying to keep his antsy body from making too much noise as they crouched behind a large English Boxwood.

Finding the mercenary camp had been far easier than he'd expected. Within an hour, they had stumbled upon a sea of cloth tents resting in a long clearing. Dozens of men weaved between them, their plates of armor clanking with each stride. The vanishing light made it difficult to count their numbers with any sort of exactness, but it was clear that a small army lay before them. Three men would stand little chance against so many.

At least not three ordinary men. Although, Eramus wasn't too keen to call Arnan anything but an arrogant simpleton. Eramus had his magic, their best weapon and hope of retrieving Evree, and Kieran had his rage and pure desire to save his daughter. Arnan only possessed a grouchy attitude and mouth that opposed Eramus at every opportunity. Perhaps asking him to come hadn't been the best idea.

"You're going to get us all killed," grumbled Arnan. "Think you know what's best just because you have—"

"Enough," said Kieran in a loud whisper. "Eramus's plan makes sense, and he is our best bet for saving Evree. If you can't accept that, then go home. I want my daughter back."

Arnan's scowl threatened to unleash a wide smirk across Eramus's lips, but he restrained himself. He needed to focus.

"Fine. What kind of distraction do you propose, *Eramus*?"

Eramus shifted. Truthfully, he wasn't as sure of himself or his plan as he wanted to be. Any number of things could go wrong, all of which put Evree in more danger, but they had to do something. He had to save her.

"Fire," he answered with a facade of confidence. "We'll set one tent on the outskirts of the camp ablaze. It will create enough of a distraction that we can slip in and find Evree."

Arnan snorted and shook his head. "That's your plan? You really think they won't notice us strolling through their camp? The moment we're spotted, they'll skewer us. Even you, with your magic, can't fight off so many."

"Which is why I brought these," said Kieran, opening the sack of supplies he'd brought with them. He pulled out several swords, two clubs, and at least six knives. Eramus lifted his brows, and Kieran shrugged. "After what happened to my wife, I swore I would never be unprepared again."

He chucked a sword towards the ground, and it landed in front of Eramus. "Take that. Even *you* might need a blade."

Besides the fact that Eramus had never actually used one, having a sword made him feel better. With his magic, he likely wouldn't need another weapon, but if nothing else, the thick metal looked intimidating sheathed at his waist.

Arnan loaded several weapons on his belt with a continued scowl and an occasional muttered insult. Eramus ignored him.

"All right," said Kieran. "Let's move to the east side of the camp. They have a few fires already going over there that we can use to light the tents. Once we do, we can look for Evree." He turned toward Eramus, his expression stoic but hope burning in his eyes. "We'll follow your lead."

Eramus rose and started forward, but after a few paces tripped over a thick tree root, nearly fumbling to the ground. Arnan scoffed. "This is already going so well. Lead us to our demise, oh great one."

Kieran shot a stern look in his brother's direction, silencing him.

They made their way slowly through the wooded area surrounding the mercenary camp, careful to avoid making any noise that would give them away. It was difficult to maneuver through the dense underbrush, but they reached their destination just as the last bit of color disappeared from the horizon. Several men sat around a campfire, their speech slurring as they dived deeper into their flasks.

"How are we going to find her?" asked Arnan. "She could be inside any of these tents. Surely you don't intend to check them all?"

"I intend to do whatever it takes to rescue her," Eramus replied without offering him so much as a glance.

Arnan groaned and pulled a knife from his waist. "I hope they are as drunk as they sound."

Kieran grabbed Eramus's shoulder, his face pale. "Finding her may not be so difficult." He pointed between two tents where a man tugged a struggling, petite form forward. Evree attempted to jerk from the man's grip and fell to the ground. He yanked her to her feet and sneered.

"Let go of me!" she shouted before he forced her into a tent and they disappeared from view.

Arnan gripped Kieran's arm, keeping him hidden in the shadows. "Don't be brash," he whispered. "We'll get her out of here." The sympathy in his tone surprised Eramus. For all his arrogance and hostility, Arnan seemed to care about his niece, but showing compassion wasn't one of his strengths.

Eramus grabbed a dry branch from the ground and pulled the hood of his cloak over his head. "I'll sneak over and light this. Once the flames catch the first tent, we'll head straight for Evree."

Kieran nodded, and Arnan sighed, but he made no retort. Eramus left them crouching behind a wide oak and made his way into the clearing. With their backs facing him, the men sitting around the campfire didn't notice his approach. Eramus lay down on his stomach and slid the branch past their feet. The piece barely reached the flames, and he held his breath that no one would see the long stick protruding between them.

Once the fire took hold, Eramus dragged the branch back to him.

"Hey! What's that?"

Eramus froze. All four men turned and stared at the flaming branch. One staggered to his feet and bent over to examine the wood. In his drunken state, the man lost his balance and smashed into the ground, face first. Eramus's stomach lurched when a pair of blue eyes met his.

"There's a man holdin' on to it!" The words came out squeaked and slurred, but clear enough the others turned to confirm. Upon spotting him, they jumped from their places on the log and staggered towards him. Eramus scrambled onto his rear and scooted backwards, but in seconds, they hovered over him.

"What do we 'ave here?" said the man with the blue eyes, pulling a long blade from his scabbard. "You're not one of us."

Without giving him a chance to respond, the man swung his sword. Eramus held up his palm, ready to cast his shield spell, but the blade clanked against metal before he could conjure his magic, crashing into another sword just above his head. Eramus glanced over his shoulder and found Kieran posed for attack and Arnan at his side.

CHAPTER SEVENTEEN
Hired for Vengeance

A little wine had a profound effect on the four men's ability to wield a sword. They staggered into their assaults clumsily, one even taking another swig before lifting his weapon. Kieran and Arnan danced around them, dodging every swing with ease. Eramus clambered to his feet and held out his hands, ready to attack.

"No, Eramus!" Kieran shouted as he ducked under one man's arm, the maneuver sending the man fumbling to the ground. "Go find Evree! We'll handle them."

Eramus hesitated. Kieran and Arnan seemed to hold their own without his help, but the commotion would draw more attention.

They couldn't fight off the entire camp without assistance.

"Stop wasting time!" said Arnan, shoving his shoulder as he ran past. "Go get Evree so we can get out of here!"

Though he hated to abandon them, he knew they were right. Eramus raced towards the tent where Evree was being held hostage, leaving behind muffled groans and clanking metal. He threw back the cloth and stormed inside. Several wooden tables framed the edges, some holding weapons and others rolls of parchment. Sacks of plundered items rested in one corner, so full a few had fallen over, spilling their contents onto the ground.

Shadows blanketed the back of the tent, but Eramus could just make out the shape of a body, huddled in the dirt and unmoving. He inched forward, whispering, "Evree?"

The figure moved, repositioning themselves but remaining silent.

"Evree, is that you?"

"Eramus?" Her soft voice sent shivers through his body. Eramus rushed towards her and crouched down. Flattening his hand, he repeated the incantation for the *illustris*, creating a blue light orb that hovered over his palm.

His spell illuminated the entire tent. Evree peered up at him with watery eyes and a quivering lip. Rope bound her hands, but she lunged forward and threw them around his neck, sobbing. Eramus wrapped his arms around her and squeezed her tight against him.

"It's all right. I've got you."

He pressed his lips against her hair as she cried into his shoulder, offering her a moment of comfort. Eramus pulled her arms back over his head and untied the rope binding her wrists. "Did they hurt you?" he asked, his trembling fingers fumbling over the tight knot.

Her answer came as a gasp. Eramus looked up just in time to see a fist smack into his jaw. He fell to the floor, and his light orb disintegrated, welcoming in the darkness. Evree's scream rang in his ears.

"Well, now. What do we have here?" A deep voice filled the space of the tent as Eramus moved to his knees. "Come to save your little lady, have you? Can't let you do that." There was a long pause, and Eramus stared up at the shadowed figure towering over him. "Say, where'd your lantern go? Had this whole tent lit up a moment ago."

Eramus rubbed his jaw. This man was in way over his head and hadn't the slightest clue what he had gotten himself into. Perhaps if he had known about the existence of magic, or that he had just punched one of the few people capable of wielding it, fear might have resonated in his voice. But his ignorance would prove useful.

Eramus sat up and held out his hands, his blue aura encompassing them both and chasing away the shadows. Color drained from the man's face and his eyes went wide. "What the blazes?"

A smirk stole over Eramus's face as he launched a wave of energy towards him. The spell collided with his chest and knocked him to the ground with a hard thud. Eramus shot to Evree's side and finished removing the rope.

"We have to get out of here," he said, pulling it away from her.

"Your fa—"

An arm wrapped around his throat, cutting off his air. He gagged and clawed at the thick muscles dragging him away from Evree.

"Let him go!" she shouted, but her pleas did nothing to convince the assailant of relinquishing his hold.

Eramus flailed his arms, hoping to scratch the man's face, but the mercenary's grip only tightened around his throat. Eramus's vision blurred, and Evree's lavender dress faded to black. In one last effort, he aimed his palm at the man's thigh and released a small pulse of magic.

The man groaned and released his hold before they both crumpled to the ground. Eramus gasped and turned to face him to fire one more blow so he and Evree could escape, but he wasn't quick enough. A cloud of dirt crashed into his face and stung his eyes. He rubbed them, but the motion only made the pain worse.

Blinded, he didn't see the kick coming until too late, and the man's foot drove into his stomach. Eramus collapsed back to the ground, gasping as a sharp pain swept through his ribs. Another hard kick stole his breath.

Evree screamed, but this time it was not one of fear. Somewhere above him, the mercenary gargled a groan. Eramus blinked until the stinging in his eyes faded. Evree's arms wrapped around the man's neck, and she held tight as he struggled to pry her away from him. He flung her to the ground, her body crashing against the sacks of plundered items with a loud bang.

"Evree!"

His aura consumed the darkness, and the energy he fired was unrestrained. The impact hurtled the man to the back of the tent, where he collided with one of the wooden tables, scattering rolls of parchment across the ground. He lay against the capsized furniture, motionless. Eramus raced to Evree's side and helped her stand.

"Are you all right?" he asked with panted breath.

She nodded, but her body trembled against his. A moan sounded from the other side of the tent, and Eramus could see the mercenary's shadowed figure moving in the darkness.

"Stay here," said Eramus, touching Evree's shoulder before making his way to where the man lay, blood gushing from the side of his head. Eramus gripped his tunic and yanked him closer with one hand while conjuring an orb of light with the other. "Who hired you?"

The man blinked at him. "I'm not telling you anything. What kind of monster are you? What is this dark power you wield?"

Heat washed over Eramus's skin, but he didn't have time to defend himself or answer the man's questions. Eramus tightened his hold, lowering his voice. "Tell me who hired you, or take your last breath."

He had never killed a man before, nor did he have any intention of doing so, but this mercenary didn't know that, and Eramus would make good use of the man's ignorance. He focused on his spell, causing the aura to increase in luminescence. The blue light reflected in the man's wide eyes, and panic flooded his expression.

"I can't! I'm as good as dead if I tell you!"

"You're as good as dead if you don't!" said Eramus, moving the light orb closer to the man's face. "Why did you plunder those villages? Who paid you to burn them?"

"No one paid me to do that...just a bit of fun along the way."

Eramus growled, his rage building. "*Explain.*"

The mercenary squirmed under Eramus's hold, his gaze fixated on the light. "Someone hired me to go after *her*!" He pointed to Evree, who sniffed at the confession. "A man in a dark cloak paid me three bags of gold to do it. Half up front, and half when I completed the job."

"Who hired you!" Eramus was losing whatever patience he had left. He needed answers, but he couldn't wait around forever to get them. More mercenaries could flood the tent at any moment, not to mention Arnan and Kieran were likely neck deep in trouble by now.

"I never knew his name...never saw his face. He kept it covered when he made me the offer. Gave me the girl's details—what she looked like, where she lived...all of it. Please! Believe me! All I know is he wanted your little lady dead."

The word reverberated through the air like the toll of a bell, sending a wave of shivers across his skin. "Dead?"

Evree gasped and wrapped her arms around herself. Eramus's pulse raced out of control. "What do you mean, dead? If he hired you to kill her, then why bring her here?" He shuddered at his words, grateful the man had decided not to do so.

"He instructed me to kill her, but I thought if I brought her back here, it would give me leverage to ask for more. Whoever this man is, he's loaded. Seemed desperate to be rid of her."

Inara's words echoed through his mind. She had said the man who took Evree had altered his plan. He had intended to kill her, but greed changed his course.

Eramus's body shook with rage. "You're telling me that not only did you intend to kill her, but you planned to see how much gold you could milk from the situation?" He shoved him hard against the ground. "You're despicable! If anyone is a monster, it's you!"

The man shielded his face, as though he expected an attack at any moment. "Please! Don't kill me! We'll leave and never come back. I swear it! Not that I have much choice now."

"How so?"

The mercenary shook his head. "This man...there was something about him. I have two decades of experience, most jobs involving revenge of some sort, but this one was different. *He* was different. Threatened my life if I failed." He drew in a deep breath and winced. "I don't know who he is, but he has power and money. He wants her dead, and now he'll want me dead, too. Hiding from someone like that is the only chance we have at surviving."

"Then I suggest you leave now. Take your men and go. If I ever see you in Izarden again, I won't hesitate to execute the man's threat myself."

The mercenary wasted no time scrambling to his feet, and in seconds, he parted the cloth, scurrying away without looking back.

Someone had hired mercenaries to kill Evree. Eramus's stomach twisted, making him nauseous. The mercenary had described the man as someone with wealth and power, and Eramus could think of only one person with motivation who held that description—King Delran.

But how had the king known about Evree? Why hadn't he come for Eramus directly? His head swirled with questions, but the most concerning was that the king must have someone watching him. It was the only plausible conclusion, and that meant Evree wasn't safe. She might never be, even if he left to Verascene.

"Eramus."

Evree's weak voice jarred him out of his thoughts. He turned to face her, and the sight of her blood-stained clothes sent his stomach into his throat. She pressed her stained hands against her waist just before her trembling body fell to the ground.

Eramus darted to her side and frantically slid his arm under her head. "Evree! Evree, please wake up!"

He shook her, but she gave no response. Blood soaked her midsection, and a wide rip in her lavender gown revealed a gash that gushed with crimson. How had he not noticed her injury before? He glanced to the plunder, noting the streaks of red coating various objects. A small dagger protruded from the pile, likely a family heirloom from a ransacked village, now covered in the fluid of death.

Evree's face paled, her lips losing their pink color, leaving them an eerie purple. Eramus placed his hands over her wound. He had to do it, but fear gripped him, making his muscles so tight his entire body ached. What if he didn't perform the spell properly? What if he couldn't remember the correct words?

He drew a deep breath. If he did nothing, he would lose her. He had to try.

Blue light flickered around his hands as he recited the words to the healing spell. Eramus watched her wound, his hope draining with every second that passed.

CHAPTER EIGHTEEN

The Escape

Each second felt like an eternity as he watched her body for any sign that his spell would work. The rise and fall of Evree's chest was so subtle, Eramus had to focus to be sure she was breathing. Blood seeped into her clothes, and he wondered if he should attempt the spell again. Perhaps he had not spoken the right incantation? What if it was too late to save her?

He placed his palms against her side and blue light encircled his hands, but before he could attempt the words, Evree's eyes flew open. She gasped, and her chest heaved under her ragged breath.

"Evree!" he shouted before leaning in close and cupping her face with his hands. "You're alive!"

"Rotten apples," she muttered, her voice hoarse. "Are you sure?

Because I feel terrible."

Eramus chuckled and glanced at her wound. Though it was difficult to see through the lingering blood, her skin pinched together in a raised scar. His spell had healed her.

Tears flowed over his cheeks as he smiled down at her. "I didn't think my magic would work. I thought..."

A large lump took up residence inside his throat. He had almost lost her, and his frantic heart still hammered with fear. Evree's eyes glazed as she sat up. She threw her arms around his neck, and for several moments, he held her tight.

When her sobs calmed, she pressed a gentle kiss against his cheek and leaned close to his ear, whispering, "I love you, Eramus."

No words could describe the warmth that spread through his body. More tears trailed over his face as his happiness overwhelmed him. With Evree by his side, he felt as though he could face the world and the prejudice against him. How could Morzaun believe love was a weakness when it made Eramus stronger? The man was wrong. Love was worth fighting for.

Eramus pulled Evree away from him and brushed a piece of her golden hair from her face. "I love you, too." The words sent another wave of warmth surging through him. Now he was certain he could never leave Evree behind. Not knowing whether she was safe would kill him, and he suspected King Delran would stop at nothing to have his revenge. Eramus would ask Kieran for her hand, and then he would take her with him to Verascene. It was the only way he could protect her; he just hoped Kieran would understand.

Eramus pressed his forehead against hers. "Do you think you

can stand? Walk? We need to get out of here."

"If it means getting far away from here, then I'll crawl if I have to."

"I would carry you before I allowed that," he said, taking her hands. "But I may need to fight off a few more mercenaries."

"I believe I can manage walking."

Eramus gently lifted her from the ground and took the sword from his scabbard. He offered it to Evree, who grimaced with hesitation. "Hold on to this," he said, placing it in her hands. "And stay close to me. We need to find Arnan and your father."

Her eyes rounded. "My...father? He came with you?"

Eramus nodded, her look of concern twisting his stomach. He'd left them for longer than he had planned, and who knew how many men had joined the fight. "Let's go. They may need my help."

Evree gripped one of his hands and held the sword with the other. The moment Eramus ripped open the cloth, smoke filled his lungs and burned his eyes. Several tents were ablaze near the edge of the clearing, and dozens of bodies scuffled past them. No one took any notice of them in their rush to escape the blackening air.

"Eramus, what's happening?" asked Evree between coughs.

He had no answer for her. Someone had set the camp on fire, and since it was part of their original plan, he suspected Arnan and Kieran were responsible. But where were they?

Eramus attempted to scout the area, but as flames consumed more tents, the smoke grew thicker. Soon, he couldn't see more than a few feet in front of him.

Evree's hand tensed as she coughed. He needed to get her out of there, away from the smoke. Arnan and Kieran would have to wait a little longer.

He tugged her forward, and Evree followed without hesitation. Eramus slowed his pace once they reached the edge of the forest. Shrouded in smoke, the dense underbrush caught his boots and sent him fumbling to the ground several times before they put enough distance between them and the camp that the air cleared.

Eramus guided her to the trunk of a pine tree. Evree dug her fingers into the bark and gasped. "My father," she said, panting. "Where is he? Where is Arnan?"

He shook his head. "I don't know. Getting you out of there was my priority. I'm going back to find them."

"You can't go back!" Evree grabbed his arm, her eyes pleading. "It's too dangerous! The smoke...and the mercenaries... What if they attack you?"

Eramus placed his hands on her shoulders and kissed her forehead. "I can't just leave them. I have to go back. Your father and uncle can't fight them all on their own. I need you to stay here. Promise me you will."

She scowled. "And what? Sit here and worry about you? That's—"

"Exactly what I want you to do." Eramus smiled and took her face between his hands. He kissed her lips before she could protest further. "I love you. Keep your sword ready. I'll be back soon."

She groaned as he walked away. "You'd better," she called after him, bringing a smile to his face.

The moment he left the forest, the thick haze burned his lungs.

Eramus pulled his tunic over his mouth and nose, hoping the thin cloth would help. He passed a few men scrambling between piles of smoldering ruin, but otherwise the camp was eerily empty. The only sound was the crackling of flames as they ate away at several larger tents, leaving any surviving material exposed.

Eramus jogged deeper into the camp. He stopped when a long groan sounded from his left. Inching his way through the smoke, he conjured his aura around one hand. The light did little to penetrate the haze, and he could barely see.

Another groan met his ears, and a wooden wagon appeared from the smog. His heart thundered against his ribs as two figures came into view.

"Confound it!"

Arnan coughed several times from where he leaned against the wheel and winced. Kieran attempted to pull him to his feet, but Arnan moaned and jerked free of his grasp. "Stop yanking on my arm!"

"If we don't get out of this smoke, your arm will be the least of your concerns," said Kieran.

Eramus rushed towards them. Blood stained Arnan's left pant leg and his sleeve around his elbow. A long scratch oozed blood above Kieran's brow, and dirt coated his skin. Their fight with the mercenaries had left a mark, but at least they were both alive.

"Eramus!" Kieran stepped forward to meet him, gripping his shoulder as he peered into his eyes. "Evree...did you find her!"

"I found her. She's safe in the forest. I came back to find you."

Arnan scoffed. "Been nice if you'd come back before they tried to slaughter me."

Eramus crouched down beside him and tried to examine his wounds, but Arnan shoved him away. "I don't need you fussing over me." He shifted on the ground, wincing again.

Kieran coughed, and Eramus abandoned any calm temperament he had left. He threw his hands onto Arnan's leg, and the man yelped, his fingers digging under Eramus's palms to pry them away. Blue light swirled around them as Eramus pressed harder to keep contact with Arnan's squirming body.

When the spell concluded, Arnan panted with pinched eyes and a deep furrow over his brow. He rubbed his hand across his leg and stared at Eramus in confusion. "What did you do?"

"Healed you. Now, if you'll quit moving, I'll take care of your arm."

Arnan drew his brows, hesitation clearly visible in his expression, but he didn't jerk away. Eramus placed his glowing palm on the inside of Arnan's elbow and repeated the incantation. Healing Evree had given him confidence, and now the words flowed with ease. In seconds, the cut sealed and a faint scar took its place.

Half stunned, Arnan examined his arm. "That's useful," he muttered.

Kieran offered him his hand and lifted him from the ground. "Let's get out of here. Lead the way, Eramus."

Eramus's lungs burned like an inferno by the time they reached the forest, and a deep cough made breathing difficult. Leaves crunched beneath their feet as they trudged through the overgrowth with nothing more than moonlight to guide them. Evree stood with both hands gripping her sword when they approached. Upon spotting them, she immediately discarded her weapon and ran to Kieran. He held her in a tight embrace, muttering in her ear.

"I suppose I owe you some gratitude." Arnan's voice came heavy, and he refused to meet Eramus's gaze. "You saved my niece, even when I thought it was impossible and foolish to go after her." His hand subconsciously rubbed over his elbow. "And you saved me as well. I could barely stand. I'm not sure I would have made it out of there."

Somewhere in those words was a hidden apology. Arnan kicked at the leaves and sighed. "You understand what I'm saying, don't you?"

Eramus fought to conceal a smirk. Perhaps it was terrible of him to taunt the man after their ordeal, but he couldn't help but find amusement in Arnan's struggle. "I'm afraid I don't understand."

Arnan growled, finally looking over at him. "Thank you."

Evree bounded to Eramus's side and threw her arms around him. She hugged him tightly, but only for a moment before pushing him away and whacking his shoulder. "You were gone too long! I was worried sick about you!"

He laughed, but it turned into a cough. Evree's face twisted with concern. "Can you use your magic to clear your lungs? Surly if it can bring me back from the brink of death, it can do that?"

"Brink of death?" Kieran stepped closer, his eyes growing wide as they darted to the dark stains on her dress.

"I'm fine, Papa," said Evree, patting his hand. "Eramus used his magic to save me."

"Then I'm even more indebted to him than I realized."

Eramus shook his head. "No one owes me anything. I'm just glad everyone escaped serious harm. As for clearing our lungs, I'm sure magic could do so easily. I suggest we wait until we are home, however. Aldeth has much more experience with healing spells than I do."

Although, today he'd certainly had his fair share of practice.

Smoke billowed behind them as they made their way through the forest. Eramus conjured the *illustris* to guide them, and soon the village came into view. Aldeth healed their remaining injuries and cleared the smoke from their lungs with the wave of his hand, but magic did little to cure Eramus's heavy exhaustion.

It took convincing to bid Evree goodnight. After everything he'd learned, the idea of letting her out of his sight tormented his mind and heart. King Delran had hired mercenaries to assassinate her, and Eramus was certain it would not be the man's last attempt at revenge. How long would it take for the king's spy to relay that the plan had failed? Did he already know?

The questions plagued his thoughts deep into the night, and sleep became a notion lost to the sounds of morning. Evree was no longer safe in Izarden. How Kieran would respond to him making an offer for her, Eramus couldn't say, but he would do everything in his power to keep her safe. Today, he would divulge his intention of marrying Evree and hope Kieran would grant his blessing.

CHAPTER NINETEEN
Truth Be Told

Though the meadow was warm and inviting, Eramus felt a sense of unease as he sat beside Evree on the dark green grass. His eyes darted along the forest edge, searching the shadows. Ever since the mercenaries invaded their village, he had suspected someone was watching him, a spy sent by the king of Izarden.

King Delran wanted revenge. Although the details of what occurred between his father and the previous ruler remained a mystery, he knew the result was King Sytal's death. His *uncle's* death. Eramus still struggled to believe royalty ran through his blood, but he had too much confirmation now to deny it.

Despite their blood relation, Delran would seize any

opportunity to kill him, of that he was sure, and the king would not hesitate to extend his threat to the people Eramus cared about. His mother, Evree...neither of them would be safe as long as Delran sat on the throne. Eramus needed to take them somewhere safe. He needed to offer for Evree's hand.

A warm touch drew his attention. Evree peered up at him with concern. "What are you thinking?" she whispered.

He averted his gaze, shifting nervously under her touch. Eramus knew he loved her, and Evree had confessed the same. Why, then, did he have no confidence in asking the question?

Evree positioned herself in front of him. Her fingers moved along his cheekbone and over his lips, flooding his body with shivers. "You're worried," she said, continuing to explore his face. "I can see it. Tell me what plagues your mind, Eramus. I know yesterday was..."

Her voice trailed away as she turned to stare out at the forest, and her eyes glazed with tears. Evree had nearly died in the mercenary camp, and the ordeal had shaken her. It had shaken *him*. Even Kieran had been reluctant to let his daughter out of his sight when Eramus came calling that morning.

Eramus tilted her chin so she met his gaze. His heart pounded hard, uncertain how she would respond, but he loved her too much to let her go, to leave her unprotected. "Marry me," he whispered.

Evree's eyes went wide."What?"

Eramus brushed her golden strands of hair behind her ear and peered into her green eyes. "You're not safe here. King Delran will stop at nothing to have his revenge. Even if I go, I fear he will not leave you alone. You mean too much to me, Evree. I could not live with myself if something happened to you. Marry me. Come with me to Verascene."

"You're asking me to leave everything I've ever known behind."

Eramus's heart raced, and he rushed his words. "I know I am, but it is the only way. I can't—"

Her fingers pressed against his lips, and she smirked. "I'm not finished. You're asking me to leave everything I've ever known behind, and yet I feel no hesitation to answer you with a resounding *yes*."

His shoulders slumped in relief, making Evree giggle. "Did you really think I would say no? Is that what had you so anxious all morning?"

"Partially, yes."

Evree leaned forward and kissed his cheek. "I can't imagine how stressed you will be to ask my father, then."

Eramus wrapped his hands around her waist and pulled her closer, a lopsided grin filling his lips. "You would taunt me about asking your father? It took some convincing, but I believe Kieran likes me. Besides, I saved your life. He couldn't possibly say no."

Her brows lifted. "And you know my father would take no issue in refusing you despite that fact."

Eramus brushed his lips over hers. "Fortunately for me"—he placed several kisses along her chin and down her neck—"he seems incapable of telling *you* no."

"And fortunately for you, I do not wish him to say no. I want to marry you. I would follow you anywhere."

"Even across the sea and treacherous waters?"

She smiled and touched her nose to his. "Across all of Virgamor and beyond." Evree pulled away, mischief in her eyes. "But I have one condition."

"Oh, do you now? And what is this condition?"

"You must bring me buttercups every day. They are your favorite, and I wish for you to always be happy."

Eramus laughed, but her words made his stomach flutter. "I only chose them because they remind me of you. I don't need flowers to be happy, not when I have you by my side."

Evree shrugged. "I want you to bring them to me, anyway. And since they remind you of me, I know I'll be on your mind."

"I assure you, I don't require flowers for that either." Evree gave him a pointed look, and he realized he was no better than Kieran. He couldn't say no to her. Eramus ran his fingers through his hair and sighed. "And what if there are no buttercups on Verascene?"

She pulled her lips to one side, thinking. "I suppose we had better plant some the moment we arrive, so you have no excuse."

He turned to his side and plucked a tiny yellow flower from the grass. Her face lit up with a smile when he offered it to her. "I accept your condition and wish to start right away."

She twirled it between her fingers and held her chin high. "Then we have a deal. How soon do you intend to ask my father?"

Eramus laughed and wrapped his arm around her shoulder. "Perhaps tonight? The sooner we leave for Verascene, the better."

Evree began plucking flowers and collecting them in a bouquet. Eramus couldn't help but watch her in awe. Her wide smile warmed his heart, and he felt like the luckiest man in Virgamor. Evree had always accepted him, even when their people had not, and he knew without a doubt he loved her.

When she couldn't hold any more, she turned to face him. "Mind helping me up?"

He lifted her from the ground, and they walked towards the village. "What are all the flowers for?" asked Eramus.

Her lips twisted into a sly smile, but she remained silent. Eramus narrowed his eyes. "You're up to something. I know that look."

She pressed the bouquet against her chest and gaped in feigned offense. "You say it as though I'm always up to mischief."

"If you're not, then tell me what the flowers are for."

Evree ignored him, increasing her pace. "I've never seen anyone so suspicious of flowers."

"Evree."

"They're for your mother. I'm going to tell her."

She knew better than to hesitate after her confession. Evree bounded down the dirt path and into the village...with Eramus on her heels.

"Evree, no! If you tell her, the entire village will know! We need to wait until I've asked your father."

Between exertion and panic, his heart beat in chaos. He wasn't ready for his mother to know. This would be even worse than when Yelene told her he'd kissed Evree. Not to mention if Kieran found out from anyone but him, he wouldn't be happy.

Eramus reached for her, but she slipped out of his fingertips, her giggles flowing behind her to meet his ears. Villagers stopped to watch them run down the path, and Eramus didn't dare call after her for fear they would find the display even more suspicious.

Evree slowed when she neared his cottage, allowing him to catch her by the waist and whirl her around. Her giggles made him laugh as she squirmed between his arms. "You can't tell her yet," he said, flicking a finger over her nose.

She lifted onto her tiptoes and kissed him. His arms loosened in response, and Evree took the opportunity to escape. "Rotten apples, I can't!"

Eramus cursed himself for smiling at her defiance. His stomach lurched when she neared the door, but before she could lift her hand to knock, it parted from the frame and Yelene stood on the threshold with a wide grin.

"Rotten dirty red apples," Eramus muttered under his breath. Did Yelene see his proposal? He thought he might be sick.

Yelene leaped forward and pulled Evree into a tight embrace. Her eyes met his over Evree's shoulder, and she gave him a wink before releasing her.

"Oh! I'm so happy to finally meet you!"

Evree blinked at her.

Yelene shook her head. "Forgive me. I'm Yelene, Eramus's aunt."

"Yes, of course," said Evree. "I met Aldeth yesterday when he healed us all."

Yelene crossed her arms and pursed her lips. Eramus chuckled. She and Evree would certainly get along fine. "I was told to stay home, and had it not been for Inara needing my company, I wouldn't have listened. But that's neither here nor there. I'm glad you've come by and I'm happy to be the first to offer you congratulations."

Evree's face contorted with confusion, and Eramus sighed. "Yelene can see the future. It's part of her abilities."

"But I haven't told the others," said Yelene, lifting her hands when Eramus flashed her a pointed look. "I wanted to give you the honor. So come inside before I completely burst."

They followed her through the door, and all hope of keeping the proposal hidden from his mother disappeared. Hopefully, his family could keep it a secret, at least until tonight when he could ask Kieran for his blessing.

Inara and Aldeth sat at the small table, but both turned their attention to them the moment they entered the cottage. Yelene bounced on her toes. She appeared ready to explode with excitement.

Evree wrapped her flower-free hand around his arm and glanced up at him, her cheeks colored. "I changed my mind. You tell her."

Inara appeared in front of them faster than a rabbit darting away from a wolf. "Tell me what?"

Her eyes suggested she already knew, and though he enjoyed teasing her with suspense, Eramus cleared his throat. "Evree has agreed to marry me."

A loud squeal filled the cottage. Eramus winced as Yelene joined his mother in complete exuberance. Inara hugged Evree so hard that flower petals littered the floor. Evree chuckled. At least she could handle his family's antics.

Aldeth placed a firm hand on Eramus's shoulder and smiled. "Congratulations to the two of you." His eyes fell on the bouquet in Evree's hand...or what remained of it. "Oh dear. Perhaps we should fix those."

He waved his hand through the air, and a green aura followed. The flower petals on the floor rose and swirled around the sad bundle in Evree's hand. Pieces reattached to stems, and the blooms opened with full beauty, a perfect display.

Evree's eyes rounded. "Oh, my! How beautiful magic can be! It amazes me every time. I still can't believe there are more people who can use it. I thought Eramus the only one until the man in the meadow said otherwise."

"Man in the meadow?" Aldeth's forehead furrowed, and Eramus's heart stopped. He still hadn't told his aunt and uncle about Morzaun and Zeeran. Something told him they would not react well to the information.

Evree tilted her head. "Has Eramus not mentioned him? He's been teaching him how to use magic. His name is Morzaun."

His uncle's reaction wasn't what he expected. Complete horror flooded his expression and Yelene gasped. Aldeth rubbed his hand over his chin. "You've met Morzaun? He's here? In the village?"

Eramus shook his head. "Not exactly. He comes to train me and then leaves. Came about a week before you and Yelene arrived."

Aldeth planted both hands on Eramus's shoulders with a tight grip. "Listen to me, Eramus. You must stay away from him. Morzaun is dangerous. You don't know what he's capable of."

Although his instincts agreed, frustration grew inside him like a noxious weed. "What exactly is he capable of? He said someone stole his magic from him. What possible threat could he be?"

Lowering his hands, Aldeth sighed. "I don't suppose he told you how he lost it? Didn't tell you who he is or what he's done?"

Eramus swallowed hard. Since the moment he'd met Morzaun, he had known the man kept secrets from him. After their last encounter, Eramus suspected Morzaun was more than just bitter about losing his power. There was something dark about him.

"Morzaun is responsible for the deaths of thousands," continued Aldeth. "He used his magic to murder the innocent and planned to bring all of Virgamor under his subjugation. Yelene and I faced him. She learned a spell that would eliminate a person's ability to use magic, and we used it on Morzaun to stop him."

Eramus shook his head. "How did he get magic in the first place? He told me the Virgàm only granted power to three children. You, Yelene, and my—"

His pulse raced. It couldn't be. His father had married a princess. He had held high rank in the king's army. The guards from his dream had called him a traitor, and Sytal had banished him when he refused to engage in war. None of that sounded like a man who would murder for power. He had to be wrong.

The sympathy in Aldeth's eyes was enough to confirm. Tears streamed down Yelene's face. "My brother was once good, full of life and light." She wrapped her arms around herself and sobbed. "But after Sytal killed your mother, he lost himself to the darkness. Revenge was all he could think about. I begged him to stop, but it was as if he became a completely different person."

The room spun. A mixture of panic and rage bubbled inside him. Everything made sense—the gentleness with which Morzaun spoke of his mother, the reason he desired to train him, and his reluctance to disclose his secrets.

The words fell over Aldeth's lips with one last whispered confirmation. "Eramus, Morzaun is your father."

CHAPTER TWENTY
Facing the Lies

Other than the sounds of bubbling water in the pot hanging over the fire in the hearth, the cottage was silent. For the last few weeks, Eramus had spent time with his father and not even realized it. Many questions flooded his mind, but one filled him with deeper frustration than all the rest.

"Why?" he asked, more to himself than to those standing near him. "Why would he conceal his identity?"

Evree placed her petite fingers on his arm. "Perhaps he's ashamed. If he has done such horrible things, he may not have wanted you to know."

"I wish that were true," said Aldeth. "But Morzaun feels no remorse for his actions. Even after he murdered Sytal and destroyed a large portion of Izarden's army, he didn't stop. He continues with his plan, and if anyone gets in his way, he takes care of them."

Aldeth's gaze flashed to Yelene, and her eyes filled with tears. Had his father tried to kill his aunt and uncle? He suspected the man had. After all, Aldeth had mentioned they fought against him, and the battle resulted in his father losing the ability to wield magic. Still, Aldeth's expression reflected more than that, an anger Eramus had never seen in his uncle's eyes. Morzaun had threatened more than just *their* lives.

"If my father no longer possesses magic, then how can he expect his plan to succeed? You said you used a spell to take away his abilities. Without magic, taking over all of Virgamor is impossible."

Aldeth ran his fingers through his light brown hair, disheveling it until it stuck up on one side. "Acting alone, yes; it would be. Subjugating everyone in Virgamor may seem impossible, but your father has convinced others to follow and assist him."

Anguish swept across his uncle's face. He bore the look of someone who'd lost a loved one. Perhaps, in a way, he had. Eramus's heart ached for Aldeth. "You mean Zeeran? My cousin?"

Aldeth met his gaze with bewilderment. "How did you know that?"

"He came once, the last time I saw Morzaun before you arrived. My father had me duel him...for practice." Although, Eramus couldn't call the fight between them helpful. Zeeran had taken pleasure in throwing Eramus to the ground and seemed far more inclined to show off than actually give him instruction.

Yelene rushed to his side and gripped his arm. "You saw Zeeran? How was he? Is...is he all right?"

Her motherly concern tore at his soul. How much time had passed since Zeeran left? And why had he chosen to abandon a family that clearly cared about his well-being?

"He looked well, as far as I could tell," he answered. Yelene sniffled, and Eramus wrapped his arm over her shoulder. "I'm sorry, but can you explain to me what happened? Why is Zeeran helping my father?"

"We don't fully understand ourselves," said Aldeth. "Both of our sons always idolized your father. He once held high a rank in Izarden's army, second only to the general. When your father refused to follow Sytal's orders, we were all banished from the kingdom. We took up residence on Verascene. The boys were young, and your father taught them to wield a sword and their magic.

"As the eldest, Ladisias received the most instruction, and by default, the most praise. I suspect that is partially why Zeeran has sided with Morzaun. He seeks the attention and recognition your father was willing to give him. Zeeran has always struggled to accept what happened and how we've been treated because of Sytal's actions. He feels your mother's death justifies your father's desire for vengeance.

"About seven months ago, we tracked down Morzaun. We confronted him and asked he turn himself in for his crimes. The last thing Yelene or I wanted to do was fight him again, and without his power, he wouldn't have stood a chance. He refused, so we attempted to subdue him, but Zeeran blocked our spell and defended your father. We haven't seen either of them since."

Everything Aldeth said made sense. Zeeran hadn't been the most friendly to Eramus when they met, and that was likely because of his father showing him so much attention. Even if Eramus hadn't understood his connection with Morzaun, Zeeran certainly had. Jealousy fueled the drive he'd seen in his cousin's eyes.

Yelene wiped her tears with the back of her hand. "What King Delran did to Feya pushed Zeeran past the breaking point, but if he knew the truth..." Her voice trailed off into sobs, leaving Eramus with more questions. How was he supposed to ask her to explain when it clearly broke her heart to do so? The last thing he wanted was to cause them more pain.

Aldeth pulled Yelene into his arms and held her tight as her tears soaked into his tunic. "Not to worry, my love. Feya is safe now, and Zeeran will find a way back to us in time." Even as he spoke the words, uncertainty filled his wrinkled expression. Aldeth was right to doubt. From the short time Eramus had spent with his cousin, he seemed content with Morzaun and eager to gain his approval.

"Is Feya your daughter?" asked Evree, her face tight with confusion. "Forgive me. It is very difficult to keep up with so much information."

Yelene ripped herself away from Aldeth, a smile pulling on her lips as she took Evree's hands in her own. "Do not apologize. I can only imagine how confusing this must all be. Yes, Feya is my youngest. The two of you will get along splendidly. She's always wanted a sister. Strauth, her husband, is new to being around magic as well, but he has been so wonderful to her."

Aldeth folded his arms and muttered under his breath. "He's wonderful to her now that he isn't holding her prisoner."

Evree's eyes went wide and Yelene turned to give him a pointed look. "That's neither here nor there. We cannot hold the past over anyone who desires to change. Regardless, what I'm saying is I think she will be happy with us on Verascene. The sooner we can leave, the—"

"We're not leaving until I talk to my father," said Eramus. And Evree's, for that matter, but not knowing when Morzaun would return made leaving even harder.

His skin burned at the thought of facing the man who had lied to him for weeks. Eramus couldn't leave without confronting him.

Aldeth shook his head. "Eramus, I told you. Your father is dangerous. You'd only be putting yourself and those you care about in danger."

"If he wanted to hurt me, he would have done so by now. I'll go alone. Evree and my mother will be safe with the two of you. I just need him to know that I've learned the truth. He wants me to join him; that's part of the reason he's insisted on training me. I need him to know I won't join his cause. I want nothing to do with him."

"Eramus, are you sure about this?" whispered Evree.

Her eyes glazed, concern etched deep in the wrinkles on her forehead. Eramus brushed away the tear that rolled down her cheek. "I have to do this. If I don't confront him now, he may never stop chasing us. Hopefully after this, we'll never have to see him again. You'll be safe with my aunt and uncle. Just promise me you won't leave their sides."

Evree nodded and wrapped her arms around his back. Eramus kissed the top of her head.

"I don't like this," said his mother. "You shouldn't go alone. Why not let—"

"I have to do this alone. I won't put anyone else in danger. Once I do, we can leave. All of us...together."

Though they all nodded in agreement, fear lingered in their expressions. Eramus headed for the door, ready to deal with the situation once and for all, but a loud gasp brought him to a halt just as his fingers slid over the knob.

He turned just in time to witness Yelene's body go limp. Aldeth caught her around the waist and guided her to the floor, keeping her head nestled against his arm. Eramus rushed to her side and crouched down. "What happened?"

"She's having a vision," replied Aldeth, his tone even as he brushed the strands of blonde hair from her face. Eramus had to give his uncle credit. Staying calm with his wife passed out in his arms would be no easy feat, but Aldeth probably had plenty of practice over the years.

Yelene's chest rose and fell with her steady breathing, but her eyes remained closed. Had he not known better, Eramus would have thought her only sleeping.

"How long do they last?" asked Eramus.

"It depends. They're all different. Sometimes only seconds; others have lasted several hours."

Hours? He didn't have hours to wait. Eramus stood and started for the door again. He needed to face his father and leave Izarden for good. That was the only way the people he cared about would remain safe.

"I'll be back soon," he said over his shoulder. "Please stay here until I return."

The small village was alive and busy in the noonday sun. He passed several wagons and a few men on their way back from the fields, their faces barely discernible through the dirt and sweat. Though the last few weeks had been difficult, Eramus knew he would miss the people he'd come to know so well over the last decade.

Eramus rounded the corner of a cottage and nearly collided with Arnan's thick form. The man held Eramus's shoulders to stabilize him, then quickly dropped them to his sides. "Eramus." Arnan stared at him for a moment before clearing his throat. "I was just on my way to see you."

"See me?"

Days ago, words like that would have made Eramus's heart race. Arnan had treated him terribly since the moment he'd revealed his power, but there was nothing threatening in Arnan's dark eyes now. Things had changed.

Arnan shifted his weight, hesitation stalling him from continuing. "I needed...there is something I wish to discuss with you."

Eramus lifted a brow. As curious as he was, now wasn't really a good time. He needed to go to the meadow and see if his father was there. The sooner he could cut ties with the man, the better. Arnan and his discussion would have to wait.

"I'm sorry, but there is something urgent I need to take care of right now."

Arnan's shoulders slumped as a mixture of relief and disappointment flooded his expression. "Very well. Just stop by when you finish...whatever it is you're doing."

Eramus shot past him, but a firm grip on his shoulder pulled him to a stop. Arnan stared deep into his eyes. The vulnerability that reflected at Eramus surprised him. He'd never seen the man look so haunted, his gaze almost pleading. "It's important, Eramus. Please come."

He released his hold on Eramus's tunic and walked away. Arnan was a hard man to understand, but ever since Eramus had saved Evree and healed him, the hostility had faded from his demeanor. Soon, Verascene would be Eramus's new home, and Arnan's grudge would hold little consequence, but he still preferred to leave his village on good terms. That included Arnan. But there were other things he had to prioritize right now.

Eramus left the edge of the village and followed the narrow dirt path to the meadow. His heart raced. There was so much he wanted to say to the man in the black cloak, the stranger who had concealed his identity to hide the misdeeds of his past.

His stomach twisted. Morzaun wasn't his father; not really. The man had been absent for his entire life and spent his own destroying innocent lives. Even though Sytal had murdered Eramus's mother, vengeance wasn't the answer. It didn't change what happened, and it would never heal the pain. His father's lust for revenge had sent him on a path into darkness, and Eramus wanted no part in it.

Dark clouds loomed overhead, and the air grew heavy. Eramus walked through the sea of colorful flowers until he reached the center of the meadow. A figure near the tree line caught his eye, and Eramus froze. Morzaun stood where sunlight met the shadows of the forest, staring in his direction. Zeeran leaned against the trunk of the oak several feet away, annoyance filling his expression.

They were waiting for him.

Eramus squared his shoulders. This conversation would likely not go well, but it was the only way he could move on. He knew the truth, but he needed to hear it from his father's own mouth. It was time for Morzaun to be honest with him, and Eramus wasn't leaving the meadow or Izarden until his father confessed to everything.

CHAPTER TWENTY ONE
The Confrontation

Dark clouds sent a wave of shadows across the meadow. The light breeze swept over Eramus's skin, cool enough to send shivers through his body. He walked towards the tree line, where Morzaun waited with his head tilted and bewilderment filling his expression. Could he sense Eramus's frustration and anger? Perhaps he could. Zeeran had mentioned Morzaun sensed his distraught before, and that's why he'd sent his cousin to talk to him until he could come himself.

Eramus stopped several feet away from his father. Zeeran didn't bother to give him even a second of his focus, but Eramus could see the irritation in his folded arms and dark eyes. According to Aldeth, Zeeran had abandoned his family, in part, because Morzaun offered him the attention his cousin wanted. Eramus had stolen some of that attention and Zeeran seemed to despise him for it, only confirming the notion.

"Eramus," said Morzaun, offering him a small nod. "It's been awhile. How are you?"

His tone sounded heavy with concern. Morzaun may have known something was amiss, but he didn't know what. Eramus suspected he might regret coming to the meadow to find out.

Eramus hesitated to answer. How did he want to approach their conversation? Right now, he was in control of what details Morzaun had, and he preferred to keep it that way. He needed to place his words carefully to avoid revealing his aunt and uncle currently occupied his cottage. There was no telling how his father might respond to their presence. Now that Eramus knew how Morzaun had lost his power and why, he didn't dare say anything that might put his family or Evree in Morzaun's crosshairs.

"I hoped I would find you here. There is something I wish to discuss with you." Eramus's gaze darted to Zeeran, who snapped a twig in two and twirled one piece around his fingers. "Preferably alone."

The words caught Zeeran's attention. He tilted his head and his eyes narrowed. "I'm certainly not leaving now, not knowing you don't want me to hear whatever discussion you're about to have."

"Are you so desperate for Morzaun's attention that you must make a nuisance of yourself?"

The twig fell to the ground and Zeeran stomped towards him. He jabbed a finger into Eramus's chest, fire burning in his eyes. "Desperate for attention? I'm not desperate for anything."

"You're clearly jealous, and only a child would act out in such a manner."

"Jealous? Of what, you?" He sneered and shoved Eramus's shoulder. "Why would I be jealous of a man who can't even use his power properly? You wouldn't last one minute in a duel against me."

"Zeeran, that's enough," said Morzaun, his voice almost a growl.

Zeeran ignored him, his face mere inches from Eramus. "Maybe we should settle this right now?"

As much as Eramus would have liked to face his cousin and wipe the smirk off his face, dueling him would be disastrous. Zeeran had far more skill and experience, and even though the man displayed a short temper and arrogant demeanor, Eramus wouldn't stand a chance against his full power.

"I don't want to fight you, and after my discussion with my *father*, he's all yours. I want nothing to do with either of you."

Color drained from Morzaun's face, and his entire body went rigid. Zeeran's brows raised to his hairline, and he backed away, holding his palms out in front of him. "On second thought, perhaps I'll let the two of you have your discussion."

Zeeran retreated towards the forest but didn't make it far before Morzaun gripped his tunic and pulled him to a halt. "Don't go far." Morzaun's eyes fell over Eramus, a hint of fear glistening in their dark color. "I need you here."

Needed him? Morzaun used Zeeran as his personal bodyguard.

Without magic to protect himself, he must have feared their conversation would spiral out of control. Morzaun feared Eramus would strike him for his lies, and he was right to proceed with caution.

Zeeran seemed to agree, judging by the wide smirk that appeared across his face. "Come now. You're not afraid of your own son, are you? Then again, without your power, I can't say I blame you. Your last duel didn't exactly end well for you, did it?"

Morzaun yanked him close and pulled his jagged dagger from inside his cloak. He held it close to Zeeran's cheek, causing panic to steal over his expression. "Watch your words, Zeeran. I may not have my magic, but that doesn't mean I can't defend myself. You know this dagger is capable of more than ripping flesh."

Eramus thought back on his earlier discussions with Morzaun. He'd mentioned magic originated from gemstones that had rained from the sky. Someone had forged several of them into what he called the Virgàm, a scepter that had gifted the ability to use magic to him, Aldeth, and Yelene as children. Others adorned items such as the dagger now placed against Zeeran's throat. The amulet allowed Morzaun to travel anywhere he chose in the blink of an eye. Whatever that dagger could do, even Zeeran feared it.

"Forgive me, Uncle," said Zeeran. "I won't disappoint you again."

Morzaun returned the dagger to the inside of his cloak and turned his attention to Eramus. His gaze fell to the ground as he sighed. "How did you find out?"

"Does it matter? I want to hear the truth from you."

His father looked up, and his eyes narrowed. "Yes, I am your father, but where your knowledge of the truth came from *does* matter. I assume you've learned more about my past, and I'd wager the details given you were rather one-sided."

"How many sides could there possibly be to murdering thousands? Innocent people lost their lives all because of your desire for vengeance. Even now, after having killed Sytal, you still speak of claiming Virgamor as your own."

"I never wanted to rule!" He stepped closer, his hands clenched at his waist. "Your mother was a princess, Eramus. Your grandfather asked me to take care of our people. He saw the evil in Sytal, in his own son, and he asked me to do whatever was needed to protect the people of Izarden. I've done that. I eliminated our greatest threat. My only regret is that I did not take care of him before he murdered your mother in cold blood."

"And what would he say about everyone else you've killed? How are you protecting our people if you wipe them out as if they mean nothing?"

"I did what had to be done! Sytal would have put us at war. He'd already attacked Dunivear and sent soldiers to Zazerene. The longer he remained in power, the more lives we lost. Yes, I am responsible for the death of many good men, but they were men who followed a tyrant who cared nothing for them, only for power. Sytal saw me as a threat, the only person capable of ending his reign, so he hunted me down and waged war against me. I realized then what I had to do. Ending Sytal's life wasn't enough. The only way Virgamor can know peace is under one ruler, someone the people will respect and obey."

Eramus shook his head. "And you think you're fit for the job? The lack of peace in Virgamor is because of my uncle. You said so yourself. Now that he's gone, why not lay this grudge to rest? You've had your vengeance, filled whatever duty you felt my grandfather bound you to. It is your selfish lust for power that fuels you now, not the concern for our people."

Morzaun's sinister laugh sent shivers down Eramus's spine. "You think the threat has vanished with the death of your uncle? Delran is just as much a tyrant as his father, and he searches for you, Eramus. He will not hesitate to kill you to exact his own vengeance, nor will he cease the pursuit of his father's vision. He rebuilds Izarden's army as we speak and prepares for war with Dunivear!"

"And your plan is no better!"

Morzaun's chest heaved, and his cheeks turned red. "Delran is a monster just like Sytal. Do you know how he killed your mother?"

Eramus took a step back. He didn't want to hear this. The few images of his mother comforting him after he'd revealed his magic were all he had of her. The last thing he wanted was that one memory tainted with the details of her death.

"She instructed her handmaiden to take you away. In the dark of night she told you goodbye, and by next morning's light, Sytal knew what she had done."

"Stop." The word came out breathless, just above a whisper.

"He demanded she tell him where she'd sent you. She refused, and he slit her throat with his sword. He left her body to rot on the palace floor! His own sister, Eramus! Your mother gave up her life to protect you. She gave up her life to stop Sytal."

A tear slid down Eramus's cheek. "And you betray her by becoming just like him. She would be ashamed of what you've become."

"Your mother made me weak. Had it not been for her, I would have ended Sytal's life long before he led Izarden to war. But I couldn't hurt her. He was the only family she had left. Love makes us weak, Eramus. It keeps us from doing what is necessary...from doing what destiny demands of us. That is why we must distance ourselves. That is why I hired someone to take care of your little distraction!"

Eramus's heart skipped a beat. "What did you say?"

Morzaun scowled. "I said, I ordered your little distraction to be taken care of, but I made the mistake of hiring those worthless buffoons who thought they could double cross me. They didn't live long enough to regret their mistake; I saw to that."

"You? You hired the mercenaries to kill Evree?"

"I hired them to keep you from making a mistake. That girl serves no purpose but to draw you away from your destiny. You belong at my side, Eramus, not here in this pathetic village playing husband. We can do so much more. We can establish peace and rule Virgamor together."

At any moment, Eramus felt like his body might burst into flames with the amount of heat radiating across his skin. His own father had hired mercenaries to assassinate the woman he loved, all because Morzaun believed love was a weakness unworthy of pursuit. Yelene and Aldeth were right. Losing Eramus's mother and the lust for vengeance had warped his father's mind beyond saving. The man before him hid a monster within, a monster that would do anything for his plan of domination to prevail.

Blue light encompassed Eramus's hands. "Darkness has consumed your soul, and I want nothing to do with you or your plan!"

Morzaun took several steps backwards. "You're making a mistake, Eramus! My plan is the only way the people of Virgamor will ever be safe. If you truly love her, then join me. Protect her by helping me eliminate the threats against us. Help me establish peace."

The luminescence around his hands increased. His father walked the line between rational and insane. Eramus couldn't allow him to continue. He threatened to destroy everything. "I won't let you do this."

Morzaun's gaze flicked to Zeeran, who's blue aura surrounded his hands. Eramus hadn't wanted to face his cousin, but so long as Morzaun lived, Virgamor would never be safe, and if stopping him required Eramus to fight, he would do so.

With all the strength he could muster, Eramus snapped his hands forward, sending a beam of magical energy barreling towards his father. Morzaun's gaze remained firm and unflinching as the light drew closer to his body.

Eramus would make sure his father's plan never came to pass. He would protect everyone he loved from the man with whom he shared a connection of blood and magic.

CHAPTER TWENTY TWO
The Fight Begins

A loud crack shook the ground. At first, Eramus thought the noise had come from the storm developing overhead, but the shimmering blue shield before him corrected the assumption. Zeeran stood just in front of Morzaun, his hands outstretched and a glowing aura dancing around them. The remnants of Eramus's attack dissipated to either side of their magical defense.

Zeeran clenched his fists, and the shield faded. "That was a mistake. You're no match for me, and I can't allow you to attack him."

"Why have you chosen to follow him? You have a family that loves you, yet you abandon them to follow a path of darkness. How can you believe that murdering the innocent will lead to peace?"

Blue light encompassed Zeeran's hands again. "What do you know of my family? Keep your nose out of where it doesn't belong."

"I know they still care about you...worry over you."

"Ah," said Morzaun, his lips twitching into a smirk. "So, my sister and her husband came to see you. They are who told you of my true identity. Tell me, are they still here? I wouldn't mind having a few words with them myself."

Eramus's stomach twisted, but he kept the fear from showing in his expression. "You won't go anywhere near them." He nodded in Zeeran's direction. "You or your guard dog."

Light flowed from Zeeran's palms, claiming the space between them. Eramus barely had time to conjure a shield before the spell collided against it. The force pressed against him with overwhelming power. Eramus groaned as his feet slid across the ground, leaving a trail of flattened grass and broken petals.

Perhaps he had made a mistake. Eramus knew facing Zeeran was a risky move, but he had to try. Allowing Morzaun to continue with his plan spelled disaster for all of Virgamor, not to mention he didn't trust his father not to come after Evree again. The idea of harming his family, even Zeeran and his father, pained Eramus, but the two of them left him no choice. The consequences of their scheme were too great to ignore.

The blue shield surrounding him flashed for a moment before the spell penetrated it. Zeeran's magical energy crashed into

Eramus's chest and threw him backwards. Eramus rolled across the grass and gasped when he finally came to a stop.

"I told you," said Zeeran, smirking. "You're no match for me. I've had years of practicing against my brother, not to mention proper instruction for incantations. You can't even remember half of your life."

Eramus pushed himself from the ground and, without a second of hesitation, fired a spell right back. The *impetras* smashed against Zeeran's flat defensive wall of magic. Zeeran laughed, which only fueled Eramus to put more energy into his spell. The effort did little good; the shield held strong.

A few more seconds and Eramus's attempt apparently lost its amusement. Zeeran growled, and the wall of magical energy flowed away from him, approaching Eramus like a giant tidal wave and smacking against him with enough force to knock the air from his lungs and topple him over. He gasped from the ground, staring up at the dark gray clouds overhead.

He couldn't keep fighting Zeeran, not when he had no chance of beating him. All he needed was a moment, one small opportunity to fire a spell at Morzaun. Without Zeeran, the man was vulnerable to magic, and even an inexperienced wielder like Eramus could take him down. None of the spells he knew were likely to do fatal damage, but if he could knock Morzaun unconscious, he could restrain him. Eramus hated the idea of turning him over to King Delran, but his father had destroyed thousands of innocent lives, and he deserved imprisonment for his crimes.

Though he didn't dare go anywhere near the palace, one word

that they had captured Morzaun would immediately bring the royal guard to the village, and Eramus was sure Delran would be more than happy to take his father off their hands. The families of those who'd lost their lives would receive justice. He just needed to be far away when the king and his men arrived. Perhaps then Delran would lay his grudge to rest.

Eramus drew a deep breath and rose. He needed to distract Zeeran long enough to launch an attack at Morzaun. He moved his hands through the air and his blue aura followed. Zeeran smiled, his expression smug. Eramus tried the *impetras* again, sending it directly towards his cousin. Zeeran blocked the attack by sending the same spell right back. His energy ate through Eramus's until it came close enough that he had to end his own and duck for cover. The stream of light flowed over his head, teasing his hair with its own breeze.

By the time Eramus stood, Zeeran had prepared another attack. His hands whirled through the air, creating particles of magical energy shaped like daggers. Eramus's eyes widened. That spell was new.

"Zeeran!" Morzaun shouted.

Eramus had little time to think. Zeeran launched the shards towards him and he conjured a shield just in time to catch the brunt of the attack. The daggers ripped through his defense, and then sliced through his clothes, leaving cuts all over his body. Eramus collapsed to the ground and groaned through the searing pain. Blood dripped from his wounds and soaked his clothing in crimson.

Eramus hugged his body. Tears trailed over his cheeks in response to the burning across every inch of his skin. Through gritted teeth, he uttered the words to the healing spell, uncertain how much damage magic could heal. Slowly, the gashes drew closed, leaving nothing more than faded white scars, and the pain subsided, though his skin tingled with the residual effects of magic.

Zeeran's cold laugh washed over him like water from a frozen stream. "Well, now. Look who's learned a new trick. I assume my father taught you that? Useful, I suppose, but not nearly as useful as a physical attack. But then again, my father isn't likely to teach you any of those. He prefers the peaceful life, even when the enemy threatens everything we have. He would bow to the will of a tyrant rather than stand up for his family."

Eramus rolled to his side. His fingers dug into the dirt as he used his elbow to prop himself up. "That's not true."

Yelene's words echoed across his mind, filling Eramus with doubt. She'd mentioned that Sytal had done something to Feya, but what, he hadn't asked. Eramus had feared recanting the details would only cause his aunt and uncle more pain, but now he wished he would have implored them to relay the details. Whatever had happened, Zeeran seemed to hold it over his father's head, and without knowing how the events unfolded, Eramus could hardly argue with his cousin. For all he knew, the man spoke the truth and Aldeth's actions justified his resentment.

Eramus pushed himself into a sitting position. His body was so drained, standing seemed impossible.

"You think you know my father," said Zeeran. "But you don't. He's a coward. He refuses to stand against Delran, even though he knows how wicked the man is. My father would rather hide us all away on Verascene, trap us on some island just because we are different. Why should we lose our freedom for something beyond our control? Why should we get punished for Sytal's actions?"

"Aldeth only wanted to protect you. He's doing what he thinks is best for his family. What Sytal did was wrong, but that doesn't justify murder. If you go through with this scheme, it makes you no better than him."

Zeeran waved his hands, and the magical daggers reappeared. Eramus's breath hitched.

Morzaun took several paces forward, but then seemed to think better of the approach. "That's enough, Zeeran!"

Ignoring the order, Zeeran extended his arm and sent the spell forward. Eramus created a blue dome to protect himself, but the strength of Zeeran's magic immediately overwhelmed him. He closed his eyes. He could feel his defense failing, and soon Zeeran's daggers would rip across his flesh again.

But they never came.

The pressure against his shield vanished. Eramus's eyes flew open. Morzaun had tackled Zeeran to the ground, and their limbs flailed wildly over the grassy meadow. Eramus took the moment to catch his breath. Using magic drained his stamina, but he willed himself to stand.

Zeeran landed a punch to Morzaun's jaw, sending him staggering nearly into the grass. Morzaun responded by barreling into his nephew, and the assault sent Zeeran over Morzaun's shoulder and down to the ground.

Morzaun and Zeeran both found their footing. Morzaun reached inside his cloak, but before he could remove what Eramus assumed was the jagged dagger, Zeeran's incantation sent blue light to encompass his body. His father groaned, frozen in place.

"Stay out of this, old man," said Zeeran between gasps.

The opportunity slipping away, Eramus zipped his hands through the air and fired a spell. Still focused on Morzaun, Zeeran did not turn to see the wave of light until just before it crashed against him. His body flung across the meadow, and he landed with a hard thud before rolling several yards.

He had to make a move while Zeeran was temporarily subdued. Eramus gathered his remaining strength and sent a beam of magic towards his father. Morzaun, freed from Zeeran's spell, lunged to the ground, dodging the attack. Eramus gasped to catch his breath. He needed to attack again before Zeeran returned, but the exertion left him breathless and dizzy.

His hands weaved through the air, but before he could complete the spell, Morzaun's arms wrapped around Eramus's waist and they both tumbled to the ground. Eramus struggled against his father, but having used up most of his strength, Morzaun pinned him to the ground.

"Stop, Eramus!" Morzaun shouted, his eyes as dark as the storm overhead.

Eramus attempted to jerk from his grasp, to no avail. "Take your hands off of me!"

"Listen to me"—Morzaun's hold tightened as Eramus ignored his command, twisting his body in an effort to escape—"listen to me, Eramus!"

Morzaun gripped Eramus's wrists so tightly they throbbed. He had enough strength to conjure his aura, but it would do him no good when he couldn't move his hands. His father, seemingly aware of that fact, kept his body positioned out of any possible line of fire of Eramus's spells.

"I am not your enemy," Morzaun continued. "Your anger is misplaced."

"You hired someone to kill Evree! That alone is enough to make you my enemy, not to mention your insane plan of domination."

"Then bring the girl if you must. It's your destiny to stand at my side."

"Never!"

Zeeran's face came into Eramus's view. He hovered over them, his chest heaving with heavy breaths. "You got one lucky shot."

"Enough, Zeeran!" Morzaun growled. "Use the *soporia*; he's coming with us whether he wants to or not."

Soporia? Another unfamiliar spell. Eramus had no idea what that particular incantation would do to him, but he refused to go down without a fight. He jerked, but Morzaun leaned over him and used his entire upper body to keep him in place.

"What are you waiting for?" Morzaun shouted to Zeeran over his shoulder.

Blue light surrounded Zeeran's hands, but his gaze had moved to the other side of the meadow where two figures ran towards them. "We've got company," he muttered.

Morzaun followed Zeeran's gaze. "I'd prefer you came without having to be knocked out, Eramus. Get rid of them and come with us, or I'll end their lives here and now."

He released his hold, and Eramus rolled onto his side. His entire body ached, but he looked up to see who had stopped Zeeran's spell. The clouded sky left shadows over their bodies, but there was no mistaking the familiar resemblance of the two brothers.

Arnan and Kieran had come to the meadow.

CHAPTER TWENTY THREE
Traitors and Tyrants

If the sky looked dark and haunted, it was nothing compared to Morzaun's expression as he watched Kieran and Arnan close the distance between them. Eramus's heart pounded so hard he thought it might break through his flesh. Having more people in Morzaun's path of destruction was the last thing he wanted. Why had Kieran and Arnan come to the meadow? Regardless, he needed an excuse to send them back to the village; their lives depended on it.

Eramus rose and brushed the grass from his trousers just as the two brothers came to a halt in front of them. Kieran's eyes darted between Zeeran and Morzaun before finally landing on Eramus. His gaze spoke without words, silently asking him if anything was amiss, but Eramus couldn't answer that question, at least not without risking the safety of the two men.

When Eramus offered no response, Kieran turned to Morzaun. "Forgive the intrusion. We've come to speak to Eramus, but I'm afraid we haven't made your acquaintance."

He spoke with all the courtesy of a gentleman, but suspicion lay hidden in his tone. Would Morzaun recognize it? How would he respond if he did? Kieran and Arnan were quick-tempered on the best of days, and Morzaun wouldn't take kindly to threats. The entire situation could explode with a single word. That wouldn't bode well for any of them, especially for those without magical abilities.

"Pleasantries are unnecessary," answered Morzaun, his expression stoic and his tone even. "We won't be here long enough for them to matter."

Kieran's eyes narrowed. "I'd prefer to know whom I'm speaking with regardless of how long you intend to stay. From what I gathered when we entered the meadow, the three of you seemed engaged in quite the tussle. Of course, Eramus knows if he is in need of assistance, there are plenty in the village more than willing to offer it."

A small nod and a wink were meant to ease Eramus's concerns, but they did the opposite. He didn't want Kieran or Arnan involved with Morzaun. The man was dangerous, and Zeeran's lack of obedience to his commands made him like a stick of dynamite, ready to explode with one wrong movement.

Morzaun scoffed. "Offer him assistance? I didn't see anyone offering him anything but banishment when he revealed his powers." He turned to face Arnan. "A banishment suggested by you, if I'm not mistaken."

"People often fear the unknown and that which they don't understand," said Kieran. "I know I speak for both of us when I say we regret the response to Eramus's abilities. He deserved better, and he's proven himself an honorable man time and again."

Morzaun smiled, but it wasn't the cheerful kind. The people of Izarden had cast his father out when Sytal marked him as a traitor, despite having done nothing to deserve those claims. That one act had pushed his father down a dark path, and Eramus guessed Morzaun had lost trust in humanity. As genuine as Eramus knew Kieran's words to be, his father would never accept them.

"How kind of you to admit your mistake." Morzaun folded his arms. "Please, don't let us keep you from speaking with my son. Your message must be important to bring you out here in this"—his eyes moved skyward—"impending inclement weather."

Kieran's eyes rounded, and Eramus winced. At one time, he'd longed to know his family and fill in the missing pages of his past, but nothing could have prepared him for the truth. Claiming Morzaun as his father meant accepting a murder's blood flowed through his veins. If it were up to Eramus, he would sever all ties with the man and never look back.

"We don't have time for this," said Arnan, his voice almost a growl.

Kieran shook his head, as if the maneuver would clear his mind. "Eramus, the army of Izarden was spotted just east of the village. Hundreds of soldiers march towards the meadow as we speak."

Eramus's heart jumped into his throat. "The army...King Delran is here?"

Arnan's brows pinched together, and he averted his gaze. "Yes."

"They've come for you," said Morzaun. "Delran seeks his revenge. He won't hesitate to put every man in that army in danger to get it. He won't care if the village and everyone in it suffers the consequences. Come with us, Eramus. It's the only way to keep them safe."

"Enough! I won't join you! I can stop his army and protect them. Delran stands no chance against magic. He's a fool to attempt such a thing."

Morzaun stepped towards him and pressed a finger into his chest. "*You're* a fool if you think you can handle them by yourself."

"This coming from the man who faced them on his own before? Who murdered thousands?"

"My magic was far stronger than yours will ever be. Mine was not the result of inheritance but came directly from the Virgàm itself, a pure exchange of magical energy that you could never match. I faced the army of Izarden alone, but as someone far better equipped than you."

"What of the others?" asked Kieran. "Your aunt and uncle would surely help protect us. Delran's army could not stand against the three of you."

Morzaun smirked, and Eramus's stomach twisted. "So, they *are* still here? How amusing."

Zeeran's expression suggested he was anything but amused. "We should go. Let them deal with Delran. This isn't our fight."

Morzaun and Zeeran broke into an argument, but Eramus hardly heard a word of it. His thoughts muddled together, processing the fact that the army of Izarden had arrived at his doorstep. But how? He'd hid from Delran, albeit unknowingly, for over a decade. How had the man discovered his whereabouts now? When Morzaun confessed to hiring the mercenaries, the notion that the king had sent spies to watch him had faded. Now he reconsidered the idea.

"I just don't understand how he found me," he muttered.

His words silenced Morzaun and Zeeran. "I'd like to know that as well," said his father. "I've gone to great measures to keep knowledge of your power contained to this village, and I don't see how word could have reached him."

Eramus decided he didn't want to know what his father meant by "great measures."

Arnan kicked at the ground, his expression even tighter than before. "I know how the king found out."

Everyone turned their attention to him, and Arnan drew a deep breath. "When we made the trip to Olgetha to deliver the apple harvest, there were soldiers. I overheard one of them talking about the king's search for a young man with the ability to wield magic. I knew they were referring to you, Eramus, and I..."

He ran his fingers through his hair, keeping his eyes on the ground. Eramus didn't need more words to understand. Arnan had sold him out; he'd told Delran exactly where he could find him.

Arnan shook his head, finally meeting Eramus's gaze. "I'm sorry, Eramus. I've acted horrendously towards you, and this...I will live with this the rest of my life. Blinded by my own hatred, I feared you would use your magic to claim a place of leadership, take away something that mattered to me. I see now how selfish I've been. The soldiers knew where to find you because I told them. Delran found out because of me, and I would take it back if I could."

Eramus had no time to react. Morzaun screamed and rushed forward. His hands wrapped around Arnan's throat and the two of them fumbled to the ground. "You! You will regret this!"

Arnan gasped and attempted to pry Morzaun's hands from his neck.

"No!" Eramus shouted. "Leave him alone!"

Eramus raced towards them, but a flash of blue light sent him rolling across the meadow. Zeeran laughed, his aura hovering in orbs over his palms. "You'll never learn."

Flailing arms moved behind Zeeran. Arnan had knocked Morzaun off of him and freed himself from his grasp. They took turns throwing punches and dodging each other's attacks.

Blue light streaked across his vision. Eramus conjured his shield just in time to protect Kieran from Zeeran's assault. "Get out of here!" said Eramus, his breathing already burdened by the exertion. "Go back to the village. Warn everyone about the soldiers!"

Eramus groaned under the force of Zeeran's spell. His shield wouldn't hold much longer. "Please, Kieran! You're not safe here!"

Kieran's hesitation only showed on his expression for the briefest of moments. "I'm not leaving you here to fight them alone. Not your father and not the army of Izarden."

Zeeran ended his spell, but only long enough to whirl his hands and create dagger-shaped shards. The sharp particles hurled towards them. Eramus shoved Kieran to the ground. The daggers shredded his shield and sliced through his clothing and across his skin. Eramus screamed as the searing pain spread throughout his body, writhing on the ground with his arms wrapped around himself.

Kieran rushed to his side. "Eramus!"

Eramus was only vaguely aware of Zeeran's approach as he muttered the incantation to the healing spell, but his cousin's words fell over him like an icy wave. "Pathetic. I don't understand why he insists on you joining us. We don't need you."

Blue light encompassed his cousin's hands. Eramus gritted his teeth as his skin stitched itself back together. He was out of time. Zeeran moved to fire his spell.

Another flash of light flickered in his peripheral. Before Eramus could process what he saw, the burning ball of fire landed just a few yards shy of them. The explosion sent Zeeran hurtling backwards and Kieran toppling over. A cloud of smoke funneled into the air as the grass caught ablaze.

The army of Izarden stood at the opposite end of the meadow— at least a thousand armed men and two trebuchets ready for battle. A second ball of fire flew through the air with a tail of flames. It crashed into the forest behind them, igniting a thick oak into a raging blaze.

Eramus caught sight of Zeeran running through the smoke. He

grabbed Morzaun—who kneeled next to Arnan—by the shoulder and yanked him to his feet. "We need to go! I won't stand against an army for you!"

Morzaun ripped from his hold as Arnan fought harder to break free. Zeeran turned his attention to the army, conjuring a spell and firing a wide burst of energy across the meadow. The soldiers lifted their shields, but the wooden piece did little to protect them, and most lay flat on the ground after the blue mist had dissipated.

Delran's voice boomed from the edge of the opposite forest. "Fire the trebuchets! Aim for the traitor!"

The surrounding grass ignited when another flaming boulder smashed into the ground. Zeeran's shield protected him and Morzaun from harm, but the smoke sent them both into a fit of coughs. They moved further from the burning grass, leaving Arnan behind.

Eramus glanced at the massive army on the other side of the meadow. They were preparing the trebuchets for another attack. Delran sat on a chestnut steed wearing heavy metal armor, his sword outstretched before him. There was no mistaking Sytal's son, even if Eramus's memories of his uncle were few.

"We have to get to Arnan before they launch another attack," said Eramus, turning to face Kieran. He nodded, and together they ran through the maze of fire and smoke.

They found Arnan flat on the ground, his blank expression staring up into the clouded sky. Kieran fell to his brother's side, his voice flooded with panic. "Arnan! Wake up, you stubborn fool!"

Blood drenched the man's tan tunic on his right side, a deep gash visible through the long rip in the cloth. Eramus's gaze flicked to his father. He stood two dozen yards away, coughing into his elbow, a blood-stained dagger in his hand.

A sharp ache stabbed at Eramus's heart as he returned his attention to the man who lay still before him. Arnan had treated him horribly and even betrayed him, but Eramus held no anger towards the man. The shame in his eyes upon his confession had been sincere. Arnan resented his behavior, and although Eramus didn't have the opportunity to say the words, he forgave him.

Kieran leaned forward, burying his face into his brother's chest and clutching handfuls of his red-stained clothes with anguished sobs.

CHAPTER TWENTY FOUR
Well-Needed Rest

Loud bangs echoed from behind them, but neither Eramus nor Kieran paid them heed. Zeeran continued to fire spells at the opposing army, but Eramus's attention rested with Arnan. Kieran examined the wound on his brother's side, tears streaking down his face.

"Can you do anything? Can you heal him?" His words, barely a whisper, stabbed Eramus's heart like a knife. Morzaun hadn't just injured Arnan; he'd murdered him. No amount of magic, at least to Eramus's knowledge, could bring a person back from death.

"He's...there isn't anything I can do for him now. I'm so sorry, Kieran. He didn't deserve this."

Kieran nodded, wiping his eyes with the back of his hand. "You're a good man to be so forgiving. When he told me what he'd done, I was so angry. I wish I could take back the things I said."

Eramus placed his hand on Kieran's shoulder. Regret was the burden of lost opportunities, one that even the most powerful and wealthy could not avoid. 'What ifs' and remorse always accompanied the loss of a loved one, especially when death took them in such devastating ways.

A whiz preceded the crash of another fiery boulder just a few feet away from them. Eramus covered his mouth, coughing as more smoke billowed from the ignited grass. The sound came again, and when Eramus glanced up, the flaming stone charged a course right for them. Before he had time to think, a flash of green light streaked across the sky, intercepting the attack. The rock collided with a shield spell and disintegrated.

"Eramus!"

Eramus turned towards Aldeth's voice. His uncle raced across the meadow, his hands encompassed with his green aura, Yelene and Evree following close behind.

Evree. Eramus's stomach churned. She was the last person he wanted in the meadow right now. Why in Virgamor had his aunt and uncle allowed her to come? He knew the answer, of course. She'd probably insisted and refused to take no for an answer. The woman was too brave for her own good, and Eramus hated himself for finding that attractive in a moment like this.

Horror stole over Kieran's expression. "Evree, what are you doing out here!"

Evree threw herself into his arms. "Papa, I was so worried when I didn't find you at home. I..." Color drained from her face as her eyes fell over Arnan's body. "Papa, is Uncle Arnan...?"

Kieran wrapped his arms around her, his tunic muffling her sobs. "I know, sweetheart. I know."

Eramus turned to Aldeth, who shook his head as if he knew what he was thinking. "No spells can change death. Even some injuries are beyond what our magic can heal."

The words were hard to accept. Deep down, Eramus had known there was nothing he could do for Arnan, but his heart had refused to give up hope. Aldeth knew magic well and what it was capable of, and his confirmation finalized Arnan's death.

Aldeth conjured a dome-shaped shield to catch another attack. The boulder crashed against it and cracked in two before landing in front of them. No matter how many attacks failed, Delran refused to give up. Eventually their magic would falter from exhaustion, and Eramus wasn't sure he had much strength left after fighting Zeeran.

"How did you know to come?" Eramus asked, swallowing hard against the lump in his throat.

"Yelene's vision. She saw Delran and his army. We came as soon as she woke up."

Eramus's gaze moved to where Zeeran deflected another assault from the trebuchet. Morzaun stood behind him, glaring not at the army of Izarden, but at Yelene and Aldeth. He remained fixated on them for several moments before turning his focus to Evree.

Eramus's stomach launched into his throat.

"Kieran, you have to get Evree out of here! She's not safe and neither are you. Both of you need to return to the village."

Evree pulled away from her father to scowl at him. "I'm not going anywhere!"

"I told you to—"

"Stay with your aunt and uncle." She lifted her chin and squared her shoulders. "I did exactly what you asked."

Eramus groaned. He closed the space between them and took her face between his hands. "Please. Go back to the village. I can't live with myself if something happens to you."

Her expression fell with a shaky exhale. "Promise me you'll be careful. Promise you'll come back to me."

He brushed his thumb across her lips, his eyes roaming her face. "I promise to do everything I can to keep you safe. I love you, Evree."

Eramus pressed a gentle kiss to the corner of her mouth, and then one to her lips. She shuddered under his touch. Sunlight fought through parted gray clouds, reflecting off of her tear-filled eyes. As much as he longed to promise his return, he couldn't. Magic was dangerous, and Delran would not back down. But if he succeeded in protecting *her*, his life would have meaning, no matter how short it may be.

"Go with your father," he whispered. "Stay safe, Evree."

Kieran wrapped his arm around her shoulder. "Come, sweetheart. Eramus is right. Neither of us is safe here. They have magic to protect themselves, and hopefully, the rest of us as well."

His brows lifted as he flashed Eramus a pointed expression. "And I expect you to come visit as soon as this is over. You and I still need to have a discussion."

Where once Eramus might have shrunk under Kieran's stone-cold gaze, he now smiled. "That we do."

Aldeth's hands glowed as his aura illuminated. "I'll keep you safe until you've left the meadow."

Kieran nodded and gently pulled Evree towards the path leading to the village. Arrows rained from the sky, clashing against Aldeth's wall of magic. Evree kept a watchful eye over her shoulder as her father guided her away, mouthing "I love you" before disappearing from Eramus's view.

A bellow drew their attention. Zeeran fired a wide wave of magical energy across the meadow. The sound of clanking metal resonated through the air as the soldiers toppled to the ground in a mess of limbs and weapons.

Yelene's hands flew to her mouth to cover her gasp. "Zeeran!"

His cousin must have recognized his mother's voice because he pivoted to face them, his eyes wide. More arrows rained from the sky as Yelene lifted the skirts of her faded yellow dress and ran several yards closer to him. "Zeeran!"

"Yelene!" Aldeth shouted, waving his hands until he summoned a ripping current of air that nearly knocked Eramus to the ground. The wind swept across the meadow, blowing against the arrows and causing them to fall short of their target. Repetitive thumps echoed as hundreds of them dropped to the ground.

Yelene choked with sobs, and tears flowed over her cheeks.

Zeeran's expression softened to one Eramus had never seen on his cousin, an almost conflicted look in his eyes. He wondered if Zeeran regretted his decision to leave or if any part of him longed to come back. Eramus knew his aunt and uncle well enough to know they would accept their son with open arms. Perhaps Yelene could persuade him to abandon Morzaun and his scheme of darkness.

"Zeeran, please come home," said Yelene, her words cut off with sniffles. "Please come home with us."

Zeeran closed his eyes, his voice quaking. "I can't."

Yelene shook her head. "Of course you can! We love you. All we want is for you to come home. This isn't who you are. You're my sweet little boy who hates parsnips and enjoys jumping in mud puddles and—"

"He isn't a child anymore," said Morzaun, clenching his fists. "Zeeran can think for himself and make his own decisions. Just because he sees things differently than you doesn't make him bad or wrong, as you would have him believe."

"Murder is wrong, Morzaun. You once believed the Virgàm gave us our power to save our people. We promised to stop the evil that plagued our land, and instead of keeping that promise, you've become the very thing we wanted to protect our people from. I know how much Senniva's death affected—"

"Don't!" Morzaun's chest heaved and fire burned in his eyes. "Don't say her name."

Yelene tilted her head, and her shoulders slumped. Morzaun moved to Zeeran's side and rested his hand on his shoulder. "Come. It's time for us to take our leave."

Aldeth conjured a shield as another fiery assault descended from the sky. Zeeran gave his mother one last frown and nodded. "Let's go."

Morzaun turned to face Eramus. "I *will* see you again, Eramus. That's a promise. Delran may not have access to Verascene, but I do. You cannot hide from me."

He pulled a leather strand from beneath his tunic and took the round object dangling from it in his hand. The amulet glowed, and within seconds, both he and Zeeran disappeared in a swirl of black dust.

Yelene crumbled to the ground. Eramus ran to her side and pulled her against him as Aldeth continued to ward off balls of fire and arrows. Her entire body shook with her soft whimpers. "He's not lost," Eramus whispered into her ear. "Not completely. I could see it in the way he looked at you. Don't give up hope."

She pulled away and patted his face. "Thank you," she said with a soft smile. "I won't ever give up hope."

"Yelene!" Aldeth yelled as a storm of arrows splattered against his green wall of magic. "I need your help, love."

His chest heaved with his heavy gasps. Aldeth could only conjure so many shields before his energy would be drained, just as Eramus's was. But what were they supposed to do? Eramus knew his aunt and uncle had no more desire to murder hundreds of soldiers than he did.

Delran's voice boomed from the tree line. "Fight back, traitors! We do not fear your power!" He outstretched his sword, his war cry piercing the air. "Attack!"

Bodies flooded across the dark green grass like a wave. Aldeth turned to face Eramus and Yelene, his eyes wide. "Yelene, we have to do something! Help me, love!"

Aldeth's words seemed to shake her from her sorrow. Yelene moved to her feet and rushed to her husband's side. She whispered something into his ear, and Aldeth gave her a nod. She sped towards the forest, and Eramus started to go after her, but Aldeth called him to a halt.

"We have a plan, Eramus. I need you to trust us. I don't want to cast any spells that could cause more damage, but I must hold them off until she is ready."

Aldeth's movements through the air were fluid, almost like water flowing through a gentle stream. When at last he thrust his palms forward, an invisible wall of air moved across the grass, the blades bending under the force.

His spell toppled half the soldiers over, but those who pushed through the current continued on. Aldeth mumbled an incantation, and the vegetation itself responded to his words. The grass between them grew thicker and taller, impeding the army's ability to march across the battlefield.

Eramus's heart raced, but he trusted his aunt and uncle. Yelene and Aldeth had no desire to harm anyone, unlike his father. Despite everything they had been through, they only desired to use their magic to help and protect those who could not do so themselves. Whatever Yelene had planned, Eramus trusted it was their best chance of ending this with the least amount of destruction and death. They wouldn't achieve peace through forced subjugation, but through hard work and perseverance. It would take both to cure the hatred and prejudice against magic, but Eramus believed they could in time, and without the loss of thousands of innocent lives.

The soldiers drew closer. Soon, they would be close enough for hand-on-hand combat.

"Come on, love," muttered Aldeth, his eyes scanning the tree line.

A wave of dark purple magic flowed over the meadow towards the army. Many of the soldiers ducked or braced themselves for the impact, but this spell didn't send them toppling over as Zeeran's had. Instead, their bodies grew limp, and they fell to the ground, completely still.

"Don't worry," said Aldeth, taking in Eramus's horrified expression. "She's only putting them to sleep. They'll wake up well-rested and good as new." He smiled, dropping his hands to his side. His shield disappeared, giving them an unobstructed view of the sea of motionless bodies on the opposite side of the meadow.

Yelene bounded out from the trees, holding her skirts as she ran towards them. "Good work," said Aldeth when she came within earshot. "That should hold them for a while."

"How long will they sleep?" asked Eramus.

Yelene bit her lip and thought for a moment. "A few hours at most. I can't say for sure, but I think it best that we're gone when they wake up. The king will return to Izarden. I don't think he'll ever stop searching for you or your father, but you will be safe on Verascene."

Safe. Eramus didn't believe there was any certainty in that, either.

His father had abandoned his attempt at convincing him for the time being, but left with a promise to see him again. Would he come to Verascene? What would he do if Eramus continued to refuse joining him? One thing Eramus *did* know for certain was that Evree would never be safe here in the village.

"I think you're right. May I ask that you help my mother pack our things? There is something I need to do first."

Yelene passed him a knowing smile. "Of course, Eramus. We'll help your mother while you speak to Kieran."

Eramus nodded and glanced to where Arnan's body lay just a few yards away. "What about Arnan? I can't...I don't want to just leave him."

Aldeth placed his hand on Eramus's shoulder. "We'll take his body back to the village. He deserves a proper burial. Go do what you need to do, and we'll meet you back at the cottage."

The battle was over, but his heart still hammered against his chest. He'd planned to talk to Kieran since this morning when he'd proposed to Evree, but that seemed like a lifetime ago. With no time to procrastinate the discussion, Eramus walked to Kieran's cottage and collected his courage to knock on the door.

CHAPTER TWENTY FIVE
A Father's Blessing

The door opened instantaneously, as if someone stood just on the other side, waiting for a knock that would announce company. Evree peeked her head around it at first, then threw her entire body onto the doorstep and into Eramus's arms. She sobbed against his chest, bringing out his own tears in response.

"I was so scared," she mumbled, gripping his tunic as though she feared he might be an illusion. "I don't know what I would have done if...oh, I can't even bear to think about it."

Eramus pressed his lips against the top of her head and smiled.

"You don't need to think about it. I'm right here—alive and well."

She pulled away, and her eyes did a quick survey of his figure. Eramus chuckled. "Are you searching for injury or just enjoying the view?"

He'd hoped to draw a blush to her cheeks, a difficult feat he'd accomplished a handful of times, but Evree only shrugged. "I'm capable of doing both simultaneously."

"I see. And are you satisfied with the results of both endeavors?"

"I'm satisfied enough to not hear the rest of this conversation." Kieran stood in the doorframe, leaning against it with folded arms.

Evree pinched her lips, but it did nothing to hide her smile. "I'm glad to see you are without injury, Eramus." She lifted onto her tips toes, her breath tickling his ear as she whispered. "And yes, I'm quite satisfied with both."

Heat crept into Eramus's cheeks.

Blast. How did she so effectively make him blush? It was hardly fair.

Evree played with the folds of his shirt, rolling them between her fingers. "What happened to the army of Izarden...and to your father? Are they still in the meadow?"

"My father and Zeeran left."

At first, Eramus had thought Morzaun afraid of facing Delran without his magic, but Zeeran's reaction to his mother's pleas offered another conclusion. Perhaps Morzaun was afraid Zeeran's commitment wavered. If given the chance, would his cousin return to his family? Would he leave Morzaun to conduct his scheme on his own? If so, that would put his father in a tough predicament.

How could he possibly take over Virgamor without magic?

"As for the army of Izarden, they remain in the meadow. Yelene cast a sleeping spell to give us time to leave. This way, no one gets hurt. I don't think Delran would have quit until every one of his men had given their lives."

"Then I should go pack," she said, pulling out of his arms. "We need to leave as soon as we can. I don't want to be here when they wake up."

Eramus grabbed her arm and drew his brows. "Evree...I need to speak with your father first." His eyes darted from her to Kieran, who stared at them with a pointed look.

Evree smirked, and Eramus's stomach twisted. "Then I'll pack *while* you speak to him. It's not as if he doesn't know what you're going to ask"—she turned to face her father and flashed him a sweet smile—"or will say no when you do."

Kieran shook his head as Evree swept past him and into the cottage. "I told you before, Eramus. When she wants something, she isn't afraid to go after it."

Eramus laughed. He'd certainly learned that was true. "You did warn me, but I'm afraid it was a warning too late to heed. She'd already stolen my heart by that point."

"Ah, yet another way in which she is like her mother—a thief of hearts." Kieran left the doorstep and nodded away from the cottage. "Come, let us take a walk. I'd prefer she at least didn't interrupt our conversation."

As dusk settled over the rows of cottages, the village rested peacefully and the two of them walked alone along the dirt path.

Eramus's pulse had gained speed again, and he wondered how he should begin the conversation. Evree may have been confident in her father granting his blessing, but Eramus was not. Kieran's acceptance of Eramus's offer would mean his daughter would no longer live in the village, and Verascene wasn't exactly a place one could visit on a whim.

"I take it I'm safe in my assumption that you have proposed to my daughter?" asked Kieran.

Eramus nodded, studying the man's expression. Kieran stared at the path ahead, revealing nothing of how he felt about the matter.

"And I'd be a fool to believe she responded with anything other than *yes*," Kieran continued. "She's had an affection for you for some time now, and it's clear my daughter cares for you deeply."

"A sentiment I return," said Eramus, hoping the confession might convince the man. "Kieran, I love your daughter. I have for a long time. She means everything to me, and I would do anything for her. I hope you know that my desire to take her hand stems from how deeply we care for each other, not some superficial attraction."

Kieran chuckled, and his expression softened. "Not to worry, Eramus. I'm very aware that your feelings for each other are real. Do you think I would have allowed you to court my daughter otherwise? I could not part with her for anything less than a man who would love her as I do and treat her with the respect she deserves. Not to mention she requires someone who can keep up with her spirit. Her liveliness can prove difficult to contain."

"Then it is good I have no intention of containing it. I love her for who she is. I could never dream of caging something so beautiful."

Kieran stopped walking and considered Eramus for a moment. A slow smile spread across his lips. "Then I give you the same answer Evree gave you. You have my permission to marry my daughter. You have my blessing. I know you are an honorable man and will take care of her. Love her. I can ask for nothing more."

Eramus sighed and averted his gaze. As much relief as Kieran's response gave him, he needed to make sure the man understood exactly what he was agreeing to. "Kieran, we—Evree and I—cannot stay here in the village. So long as my father remains free, she will never be safe."

Kieran's brows tightened. "What do you mean? Clearly, your father takes no issue with violence, but I fail to see why he would hold a grudge against Evree. Surely you don't intend to allow him into your life after what he did to Arnan?"

Eramus wet his lips. The idea of telling Kieran the things he had learned the past day only sent his heart racing again. "No, I want nothing to do with my father. There is so much you don't know or understand. I wish I could explain everything to you, Kieran, but I fear it would only put you in danger as well. The less you know, the better. But you deserve to know the truth of Evree's capture. The mercenaries targeted her because my father hired them. He believes Evree is a distraction, that love is nothing more than a weakness that would keep me from standing at his side.

"He instructed the mercenaries to kill her, but they thought to demand more compensation and kidnapped her instead. We are fortunate that man is subject to such greed, at least in this case."

Kieran ran his fingers through his hair. "You believe if you remain here, your father will come for her again? What makes you think she'll be any safer if you leave? He tracked you down once; he could do so again."

"He can, and truthfully, he knows where I intend to go. But at least on Verascene magic can protect her. My aunt and uncle, my cousins...we will all protect her."

"Verascene?" Kieran folded his arms. His dark eyes filled with understanding and a painful sorrow flooded his expression. "The unreachable island. If you go there, if I accept your offer for my daughter's hand, I may never see her again. This is what you wish me to know. You think I may change my mind, knowing I am losing her completely."

Eramus kicked at the ground, the guilt caused by Kieran's words eating away at him. Kieran placed a hand on Eramus's shoulder. "But how can I change my mind, knowing doing so would put her at risk? I trust you to take care of my daughter, Eramus. I trust you to protect her, especially if I cannot do it myself."

"You could come with us," Eramus said, meeting his gaze. "You could come to Verascene, and then you would not lose her. I know she—"

Kieran held up his hand and shook his head. "My place is here."

"But—"

"I can't, Eramus." Kieran rubbed his hand over his face before pressing his mouth against fist. "I once made promises, too—to love and to protect. I failed to keep them, and that failure cost me the person I loved most. She's buried in the meadow, Eramus. And though my wife has departed this world, I cannot bring myself to abandon her. I cannot leave this village.

"You and Evree are beginning a life and journey of your own, and I have every assurance you will cherish and protect her. Besides, with my brother's death, it is time I accept new responsibilities. The people will need someone to guide them, and your mother has insisted that is my place for some time."

Eramus laughed. "She will be happy to hear you intend to accept the role."

Kieran turned, and together they walked towards his cottage. They continued several yards before Eramus continued, "I can't make you any promises, but I will do my best to find a way for Evree to keep in touch with you."

"Keep in touch?" Kieran said with a chuckle. "How do you intend to achieve such a thing living on an island no one can get to? I don't believe messengers do much traveling there."

"Perhaps not, but as I've learned the past few weeks, magic is capable of more than I ever imagined. Aldeth may know a way."

"Then I offer you my gratitude should you discover it, but if not, I will rest well knowing my daughter is happy and safe with you."

They stopped outside of Kieran's cottage. Evree stood with her forehead pressed against the window, but disappeared the moment she saw them. The door swung open, and Evree bounded outside. Her eyes darted from Kieran to Eramus, and she bounced with anticipation.

"Well?" she said when neither of them spoke.

Eramus offered her a fake scowl. "I thought you were confident your father would grant me his blessing?"

She tilted her head, and sunlight glistened off her brilliant green eyes. "Confidence does not guarantee success, sir, even for someone as confident as me."

Kieran laughed and stepped towards her. His hands fell on both of her shoulders, his eyes glazing over. "Yes, sweetheart. I've granted you both my blessing."

Evree giggled and kissed her father's cheek before leaping around him to throw herself into Eramus's arms. He wrapped them around her and pulled her against his chest.

"I'm so happy," she whispered. "I love you."

Eramus lifted her from the ground and spun in a circle, inciting more giggles from the woman he loved. "I love you, too. And I can't wait to spend the rest of my life with you."

She smirked, and Eramus's stomach fluttered. "So we'll have the wedding soon, then? Seeing as how you can't wait?"

"As soon as possible. Although, my aunt may make a spectacle of the whole thing."

She shrugged, but her smile never faded. "I think I can handle that, so long as I have you."

And she would. He would stand by her side until the day he died. Evree gave him purpose, and he would protect her with every ounce of strength he possessed, whether it from armies of mighty kings or threats of magic. Love would always be worth fighting for, a notion long lost to his father. Love would be Eramus's strength to fight whatever Morzaun brought his way.

CHAPTER TWENTY SIX
New Beginnings

"Do you have your letter?" asked Eramus, sneaking a glance at his wife as she pulled a brush through her long, golden hair. He never grew tired of watching her. Brushing her hair, cooking, chasing the chickens—it didn't matter. Her every movement made him smile and drew him in.

"I do," she answered.

Eramus couldn't see her face with her back towards him, but he could hear the smile in her tone. He'd earn a good one if she ever finished and turned around. He played with the smooth stems behind his back, rolling them anxiously between his fingers.

"Very good. I'm sure your father will be glad to hear from you."

She moved the brush to the other side of her head. "You say it as though I haven't written to him three times this week. Aldeth may grow tired of ensuring our correspondence at this rate. I should probably cut back. I don't wish to be a burden."

As promised, Eramus had asked Aldeth if there was a way for Evree to write to her father. Human messengers from Verascene were nonexistent, but Aldeth's unique abilities held the solution. As an Elementalist, his uncle had control over wind, water, fire, and the earth. But what Eramus hadn't known was that Aldeth possessed a deep connection to nature and animals. In one wave of his hand, he'd convinced a cute, yellow-breasted warbler to make the long flight to deliver a letter to Kieran. Then the animal had waited for Kieran to respond with one of his own.

According to his first letter, it had taken Kieran a few days to understand what the insistent creature wanted. He mentioned it had pecked at his bedroom window the entire first night and made laps around his head while he worked the next day. The animal had made enough of a scene to send the entire village into an uproar of superstitions, but once Kieran realized what the bird wanted, the subsequent letters had returned much faster.

"You're not a burden to anyone, Evree. Aldeth does not mind sending your letters. It only requires a few seconds of his time. If I had the ability to do it myself, I would."

She sighed and set the brush down on the small desk in front of her. "Yes, I know. Speaking of your abilities, how did training go today?"

Eramus cleared his throat. For the last week, his cousin, Ladisias, had been training him, but today Eramus had asked to forgo practicing spells. He had a promise to keep, and he refused to let another day go by without fulfilling it. Ladisias, of course, had given him an odd look at the request, but found the whole thing amusing once Eramus explained the situation.

"It went well," he answered.

It wasn't a lie. His day had gone well, even if it had taken him and his cousin four hours to find a flower.

Evree turned to face him and his breath caught. Her green dress matched her eyes and accentuated her figure in ways that made his heart pound. Golden strands of hair fell over her shoulders, nearly down to her waist, and that smile—it made his stomach flutter. At least it did until it disappeared.

She scowled, which didn't make her any less attractive. "Must you stand there gawking at me that way? It makes me so...self conscious." She muttered the last bit, just as a rosy tint entered her cheeks.

Eramus grinned at his victory. "It's not my fault you're beautiful. And, as your husband, it is well within my rights to gawk at you whenever I wish."

She fought a smile as she stepped towards him, bringing with her the smell of lavender. "Then I suggest, *husband,* that you get all your gawking done now. I don't want you staring embarrassingly at me while we are at your aunt's and uncle's."

Eramus scoffed. "As if I'd be the only man fixated on his wife. Strauth and Feya are ten times worse. The way they stare at each other makes everyone in the room uncomfortable."

Evree covered her giggle with her hand. "Perhaps it is a symptom of being with child. They *are* expecting their first. Strauth adores her, round belly and all."

His gaze dropped to his wife's stomach, and he couldn't help but imagine how adorable she would be as a walking melon. Evree whacked his arm and chided him with her eyes as though she could hear his thoughts. "Stop that right now. We've only been married for two weeks."

"Speaking of which, I hope you'll forgive me for being a little behind." He pulled a bouquet of buttercups from behind his back and flashed the most charming grin he could muster. "These were very difficult to find, I'll have you know. And my cousin may think I'm insane for requesting his help on my quest."

Evree took them from him and buried her nose into the blooms, closing her eyes as she drew in their sweet scent. "They're lovely. Thank you."

"We'll need to plant some closer to home. That hike might kill me when I'm old and decrepit."

She laughed, and Eramus took pleasure in the sound. A long hike would be worth every smile and giggle the small yellow flowers produced.

"I'll put these in a vase while you go change for dinner," she said. "Your clothes are filthy."

Eramus nodded and followed his wife's instructions. Minutes later, her arm wrapped around his as they walked the short distance to Aldeth's and Yelene's cottage. Warm, salty air filled his lungs, despite the sun having disappeared behind the lone peak in the distance. A light breeze teased at Evree's hair, and the call of crickets became the music of the night.

Light footsteps followed three taps on the door. Yelene appeared in the frame, gesturing them inside with a warm smile. Aldeth sat at a long table, Ladisias to one side and Feya the other. Strauth leaned close from her other side, whispering in her ear.

Feya's eyes rounded as she turned her attention to Eramus and Evree. "Oh! The newlyweds are finally here!"

"Good," said Ladisias. "My stomach says you're late."

Feya glared at him. "Hush, Ladisias. When you finally fall in love, you'll understand there are many things that can make one late to dinner, especially the weeks following a wedding." She flashed Eramus a mischievous smile and a wink.

Heat rushed up the back of his neck and into his ears. Feya's exuberance exceeded Yelene's, something Eramus thought impossible until he met his cousin. However, he suspected Feya's excitement was, in part, because she now had a sister. She and Evree had spent hours together already, and his wife likely knew his cousin better than he did.

"Well, don't stand about," said Yelene, giving him and Evree a gentle push on the back. "Come sit down."

Inara appeared from the tiny kitchen, carrying a basket of fresh-baked bread. Eramus's stomach grumbled as his mother passed by him, wafting the smell into his nostrils. Catching his expression, Ladisias chuckled. "Now you know how I've felt the last hour. Try sitting in here while Inara and mother cook. It's nothing short of torture."

Eramus agreed. Before their marriage, he and Evree had lived with his aunt and uncle for a week, dealing with the tantalizing dinner smells each evening would bring while they constructed a cottage of their own. Magic had assisted in the quick building of his new home, a fact he was grateful for. Not only had he wanted to marry Evree as soon as possible, but living in this cramped space with so many people had overwhelmed him. Aldeth and Yelene had started on a cottage for his mother as well; soon she would have a place of her own, right next to them.

They all gathered around the table and partook of the delicious meal before them. Not so long ago, Eramus had only Inara to call family, but now his life and heart were full. The smiling faces and laughter flooded his soul with warmth.

"Feya, have you and Strauth decided on any names?" asked Evree, setting her fork on her empty plate.

"Not completely. We still don't have a name for a girl, but I think we've settled on one for a boy."

Yelene wiggled in her chair, the suspense clearly more than she could bear. "Oh! Please tell us."

Feya looked to Strauth, and wide grins stole over both of their faces. They were having one of their moments again. The world around them apparently melted away as they passed each other adoring looks. Eramus bit his lip to contain a chuckle and elbowed Evree in the side. She smacked his leg and gave him a disapproving frown.

Ladisias held a fist to his mouth and cleared his throat...loudly.

"We've decided to name a son after Strauth's father," said Feya, ignoring her brother's teasing smirk. "Fyord, for a boy."

Yelene sighed, her eyes glazing over. "What a wonderful way to honor the general."

Eramus turned to face her. The general? Strauth's father had been a general? The new information made his stomach twist. His father had held rank in Izarden's army, one just below the general, and Eramus couldn't help but wonder if Strauth's father had known his own. It was another question to store in his pocket until he could talk to Yelene. He hadn't dared to breach the subject with Aldeth around. His uncle seemed uninterested in discussing anything to do with Strauth, a clear resentment towards the man married to his daughter and one that Eramus didn't understand.

Aldeth ran his fingers through his hair and smiled, although Eramus could tell he forced the expression. "That's wonderful, Feya. General Fyord was a good man."

Strauth averted his gaze and rubbed his hand over his mouth. Whatever animosity existed between them, Eramus could see it bothered the man. Why Aldeth, someone he knew to be kind and slow to anger, would find contempt with Strauth, he didn't know.

But he would find out.

The questions had eaten away at him long enough. He just needed to speak with Yelene alone.

Eramus leaned towards Evree. "You should have Aldeth send off your letter. It's getting late."

Evree turned to face Aldeth, and her unspoken request brought an immediate smile to his face. "Of course. We can go right now."

He rose, and Evree moved to follow him, but Eramus's soft

touch on her arm made her pause. "I'll join you in a little while. I'd like to speak with my aunt."

His gaze flicked to Yelene. She'd heard him, and judging by the small nod she returned, she knew what he wanted. He needed answers. As much as he'd come to know about his father's past, there were still details requiring clarity.

Strauth stood and held out his hand to his wife. "We should get home. Feya needs to rest."

Feya scowled at him. "Just because I'm with child doesn't mean I need to sleep all day. I can handle dinner with my family."

"Oh, you certainly handled dinner just fine," said Ladisias, swiping his light brown hair from his eyes. "I think you ate twice the amount of everyone else."

Feya ignored him.

"Then how about an evening walk with your husband?" Strauth asked, offering her his hand again with a lopsided smile.

To that, she answered with a grin and accepted his hand. Feya held her rounded belly as he lifted her from the chair. "Goodnight everyone," she said with a cheerful wave.

Ladisias leaned onto the table and propped his chin onto his fist. "Don't pop on the way home."

Feya stopped at the door and glared at him. "If you don't stop teasing me, I'll pop *you*...right in the nose."

Eramus laughed, remembering how Evree had once considered doing the same to Morzaun. It was no wonder the two of them got along so well.

Ladisias chuckled, and a screech sounded through the cottage as his chair slid against the floor. "Well, I believe I shall turn in for the night. Searching for flowers is rather exhausting work." He passed Eramus a wink before disappearing through the door.

"I'm going to turn in as well," said Inara. She gave Eramus a kiss on the cheek before exiting the room, leaving him and Yelene alone at last.

Yelene stared at Eramus with raised brows. "I'm curious about the flowers, but I will hold my questions for another time. I sense you have quite a few of your own."

"I do, and I hope you don't think I'm too forward for asking. I'd like to know why Aldeth struggles to accept Strauth. Has he done something to offend him? Or does it have something to do with his father?"

Her sigh fell heavy with her slumped shoulders. "You mean because Strauth's father was the general of Izarden? I assumed you would want to know more about that, and to answer your unspoken question...yes, your father knew Strauth's father. Aldeth and I did as well. We met him shortly after receiving our powers. He was a good man, an ally. General Fyord is the one who discovered that Sytal was behind many wicked acts against his own kingdom.

"But that is information for another time. Aldeth's struggle isn't with the former general, but with Strauth himself. You see, Strauth wasn't always the man you've come to know him to be. He hated magic and anyone who could wield it."

Eramus shook his head. "That doesn't make sense. How could he marry Feya if he hates magic? Surely he knew of her power before they wed?"

"He certainly did, but love has a way of changing people." The soft smile faded from her lips. "Your uncle struggles to forgive Strauth of his past misdeeds. Feya nearly lost her life on multiple occasions, and Strauth had a hand in that. I suspect he's afraid to trust him, but I know he'll come around, eventually."

Eramus massaged his throbbing forehead. Was every aspect of his family's past complicated? "Are you saying Strauth threatened to kill Feya, or even attempted to?"

Yelene chuckled, which didn't seem an appropriate response to Eramus. "Yes to both, I suppose." She took in his bewilderment with another laugh. "Perhaps I should start from the beginning."

She moved from her chair across the table and sat down next to him.

"Allow me to tell you a story of love and magic."

Thank you for reading! If you enjoyed this book, please consider leaving me a review on Amazon! Book 2 coming soon!

Want more? Visit my website www.brookejlosee.com for character art, excerpts, and more! You can also sign up for my monthly newsletter to get *The Prisoner of Magic* for absolutely free! Just follow this link:

https://bit.ly/VirgamorMessenger

Titles in this series:

Blood & Magic
Love & Magic
Revenge & Magic
War & Magic

Want more stories from this magical world? Check out
my other books!

The Prisoner of Magic
The Witch of Selvenor
The Warlock of Dunivear
Origins of Virgàm
The Seer of Verascene
Shadows of Aknar
Path to Irrilàm
The Sorcerer of Kantinar

Acknowledgments

Writing a book requires a team, and I am ever so fortunate to have the best people by my side to help me every step of the way. A big shout out to all those involved in getting this book on the shelves—to you I owe so much. Thank you!

To my wonderful husband, who not only encourages me to continue, but also assists in making my covers. To my beta readers, Justena White and Michelle Dawn, who's invaluable feedback helped me continually improve and make this story even stronger. To Jake and Mindy Porter for always providing helpful insight and encouragement. To Kaybree Cowley, my number one fan who's demands for the next chapter keep me going. And to all those who continue to support me on this writing adventure, thank you.

ABOUT THE AUTHOR

Brooke Losee lives in Utah with her husband and three children. She enjoys writing, gardening, rock hounding, and just being a *mom*. Brooke appreciates the small town lifestyle and adventurous landscapes of where she lives, often using her background in Geology to aid in her writing. She has always had a passion for science, history, and of course, all things books.